KONOSUBA: an EXPLOSION on this WONDERFUL WORLD!

MEGUMIN'S TURN

My name is Funifura, first of the filial-minded of the Crimson Magic Clan, and she who is called "Bro-con"! ...Bro-con...

My name is Dodonko, the Crimson Magic Clan's number one... number one...what was it again?

M-my name is Yunyun... She who will one day be chief of the Crimson Magic Clan...

My name is Nerimaki, number one brewer's daughter of the Crimson Magic Clan and she who shall one day run the brewery!

My name is Arue. Maturest among the Crimson Magic Clan and she who aims to be an author!

Yunyun, don't shove!

My name is Megumin! First among the geniuses of the Crimson Magic Clan and lover of Explosion!

My name is Komekko! She who is entrusted with watching the house, and slyest demon of the little sisters of the Crimson Magic Clan!

KONOSUBA: AN EXPLOSION ON THIS WONDERFUL WORLD! MEGUMIN'S TURN

1

NATSUME AKATSUKI

ILLUSTRATION BY
KURONE MISHIMA

YEN ON
NEW YORK

KONOSUBA: AN EXPLOSION ON THIS WONDERFUL WORLD!

1

NATSUME AKATSUKI

Translation by Kevin Steinbach
Cover art by Kurone Mishima

KONO SUBARASHI SEKAI NI SHUKUFUKU WO! SPIN OFF · KONO SUBARASHI SEKAI NI BAKUEN WO! Vol. 1
MEGUMIN NO TURN
© Natsume Akatsuki, Kurone Mishima 2014
First published in Japan in 2014 by KADOKAWA CORPORATION, Tokyo.
English translation rights arranged with KADOKAWA CORPORATION, Tokyo, through TUTTLE-MORI AGENCY, INC., Tokyo.

English translation © 2019 by Yen Press, LLC

Yen On
150 West 30th Street, 19th Floor
New York, NY 10001

Visit us at yenpress.com
facebook.com/yenpress
twitter.com/yenpress
yenpress.tumblr.com
instagram.com/yenpress

First Yen On Edition: December 2019

Yen On is an imprint of Yen Press, LLC.
The Yen On name and logo are trademarks of Yen Press, LLC.

The publisher is not responsible for websites (or their content) that are not owned by the publisher.

Library of Congress Cataloging-in-Publication Data
Names: Akatsuki, Natsume, author. | Mishima, Kurone, 1991– illustrator. | Steinbach, Kevin, translator.
Title: Konosuba, an explosion on this wonderful world! / Natsume Akatsuki ; illustration by Kurone Mishima ; translation by Kevin Steinbach ; cover art by Kurone Mishima.
Other titles: Kono subarashii sekai ni bakuen wo! (Light novel). English
Description: First Yen On edition. | New York, NY : Yen On, 2019.
Identifiers: LCCN 2019038569 | ISBN 9781975359607 (v. 1 ; trade paperback)
Subjects: CYAC: Fantasy. | Magic—Fiction. | Future life—Fiction.
Classification: LCC PZ7.1.A38 Km 2019 | DDC 741.5/952—dc23
LC record available at https://lccn.loc.gov/2019038569

ISBNs: 978-1-9753-5960-7 (paperback)
978-1-9753-8701-3 (ebook)

10 9 8 7 6 5 4 3 2 1

LSC-C

Printed in the United States of America

CRIMSON MAGIC VILLAGE: ETERNAL GUIDE

Descriptions & pictures: Arue

SIGHTSEEING GUIDE

Even the Demon King fears our Crimson Magic Village, but you don't have to fear our plethora of fine tourist destinations! There are powerful magic creatures in the wilderness—so take caution when making your trip!

▶ Wishing Pond

Holy pond. Offer an ax to summon the goddess of gold and silver or toss in a coin to make your wish come true!

▶ Stone with a Sword in It

A legendary sword is lodged in this rock. It's said whoever pulls it out will be given great power.

▶ Public Bath "Mixed Bath"

A dynamic hot bath where the owner uses Create Water to keep the tub full and Fireball to heat it.

▶ The Deadly Poison Café

Featuring food as fine as its name. One of sever▮ must-see shop▮ adored by fans of the village, along▮ with our arm▮ shop, Goblin Slayer.

Check it out!

The Crimson Magic Village is full of top Arch-wizard talents. Who knows? Maybe the one to defeat the Demon King will come from this very town!

Diagram of Crimson Magic Village School

Hallway/Entrance							Courtyard
	Fuuifura	Student C	Student B	Student A	Yunyun	Megumin	Window
Exit	Nerimaki	Dodonko	Sakiberii	Koikoi	Arue		Window
			Pucchin	Lectern			

One-on-One Interview with "Crimson Magic Village School's Number One Genius"!

Correct.
I am the number one genius at Crimson Magic Village School.
I seek to be the strongest. I have no interest in mere advanced magic.

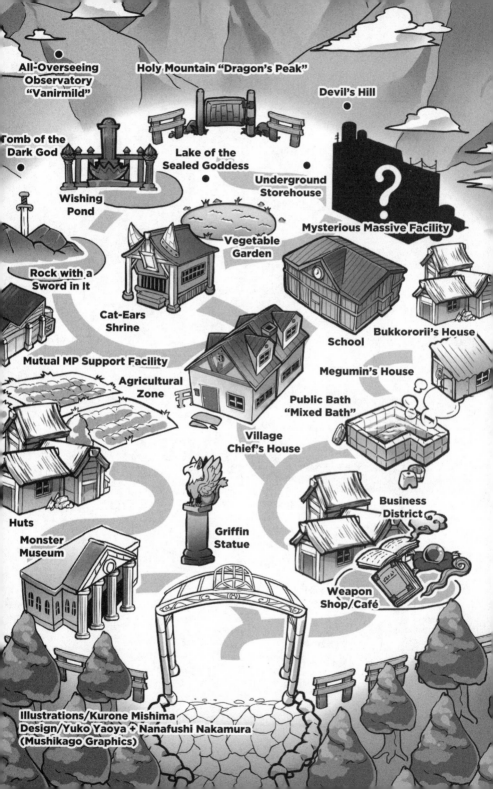

All-Overseeing Observatory "Vanirmild"

Holy Mountain "Dragon's Peak"

Devil's Hill

Tomb of the Dark God

Lake of the Sealed Goddess

Underground Storehouse

Wishing Pond

Mysterious Massive Facility

Vegetable Garden

?

Rock with a Sword in It

Cat-Ears Shrine

School

Bukkororii's House

Mutual MP Support Facility

Agricultural Zone

Megumin's House

Public Bath "Mixed Bath"

Village Chief's House

Business District

Huts

Monster Museum

Griffin Statue

Weapon Shop/Café

Illustrations/Kurone Mishima
Design/Yuko Yaoya + Nanafushi Nakamura
(Mushikago Graphics)

KONOSUBA: AN EXPLOSION ON THIS WONDERFUL WORLD!

CONTENTS

Prologue

*"**Explooosion!**"*

Someone with a hood concealing their face incanted the spell quietly.

As soft as their voice was, though, the magic that was unleashed was tremendously powerful. A roar shook the air, and a blistering wind surged in every direction. The big, black monster that had been chasing me was easily blown away by it.

But the spell, infused with tons of MP, didn't stop there—no, it decimated my sacred play area, and the toy I'd been so lucky to find vanished without a trace.

All of it was simply swept away by the power.

It was a level of destruction far beyond any other magic. To think a single wizard with a single spell could summon up such extensive devastation.

But what spell *was* it?

I had never seen any of the grown-ups in the village use such awesome magic.

The person in the hood walked over to where I was standing, dumbfounded with amazement.

"Are you all right? You're not hurt, are you?"

*　　*　　*

The person knelt down so they were peering into my face. The drab robe mostly hid their body from view, but the act of crouching down emphasized a very large chest.

...*Incredible.*

The magic spell had been amazing, sure, but this was even more impressive!

"How can I get to be like you, miss?" I didn't even say thank you, just voiced the first thing that came to my mind.

My mother had said something recently that I couldn't get out of my head:

"The women of our household have had modest proportions for generations, so just give up already."

But I wouldn't give up.

Not till the bitter end.

I clenched my fist with this private resolution as I stared at the figure's most striking attribute...

I almost felt like the hooded woman was smiling at me.

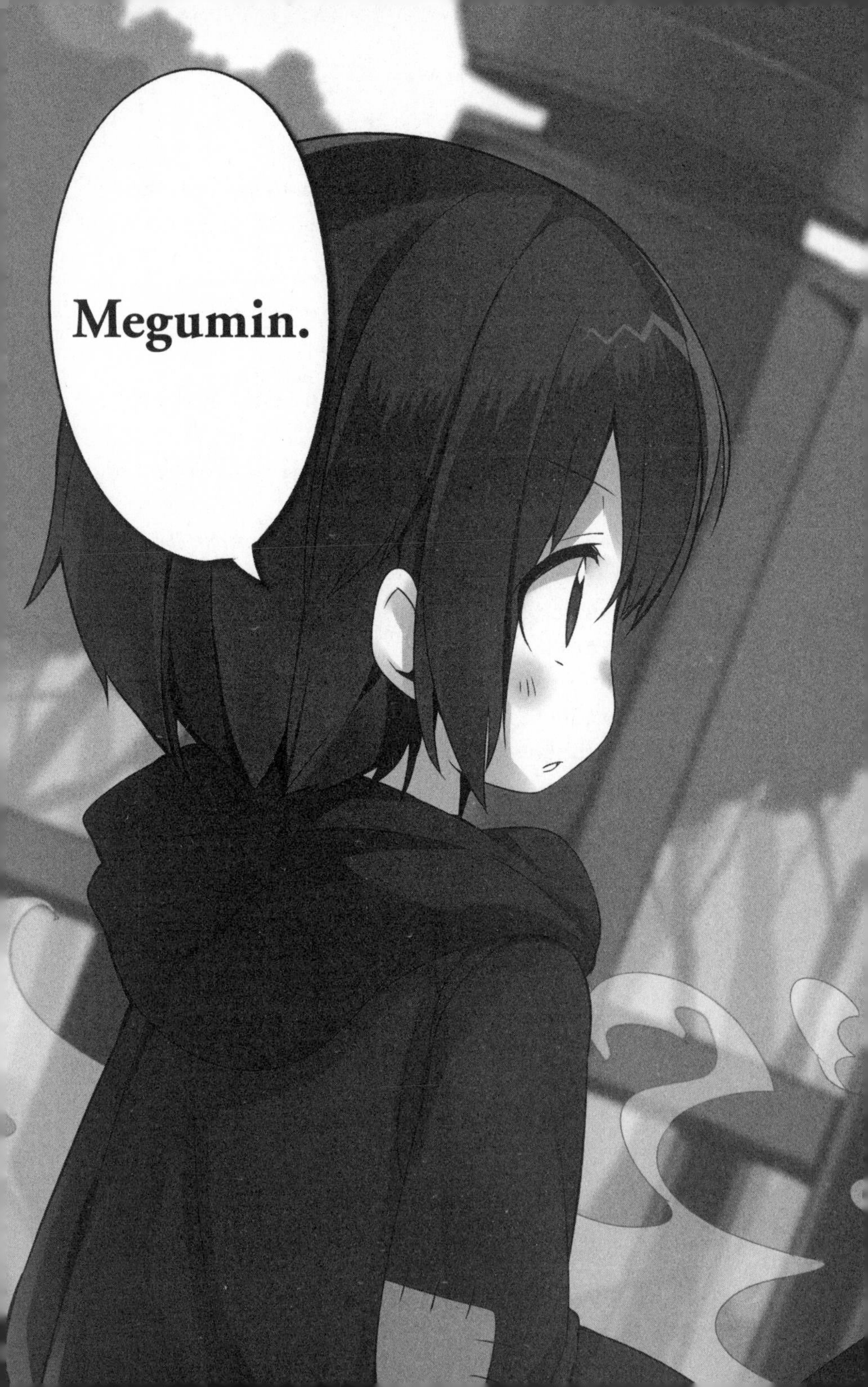
Megumin.

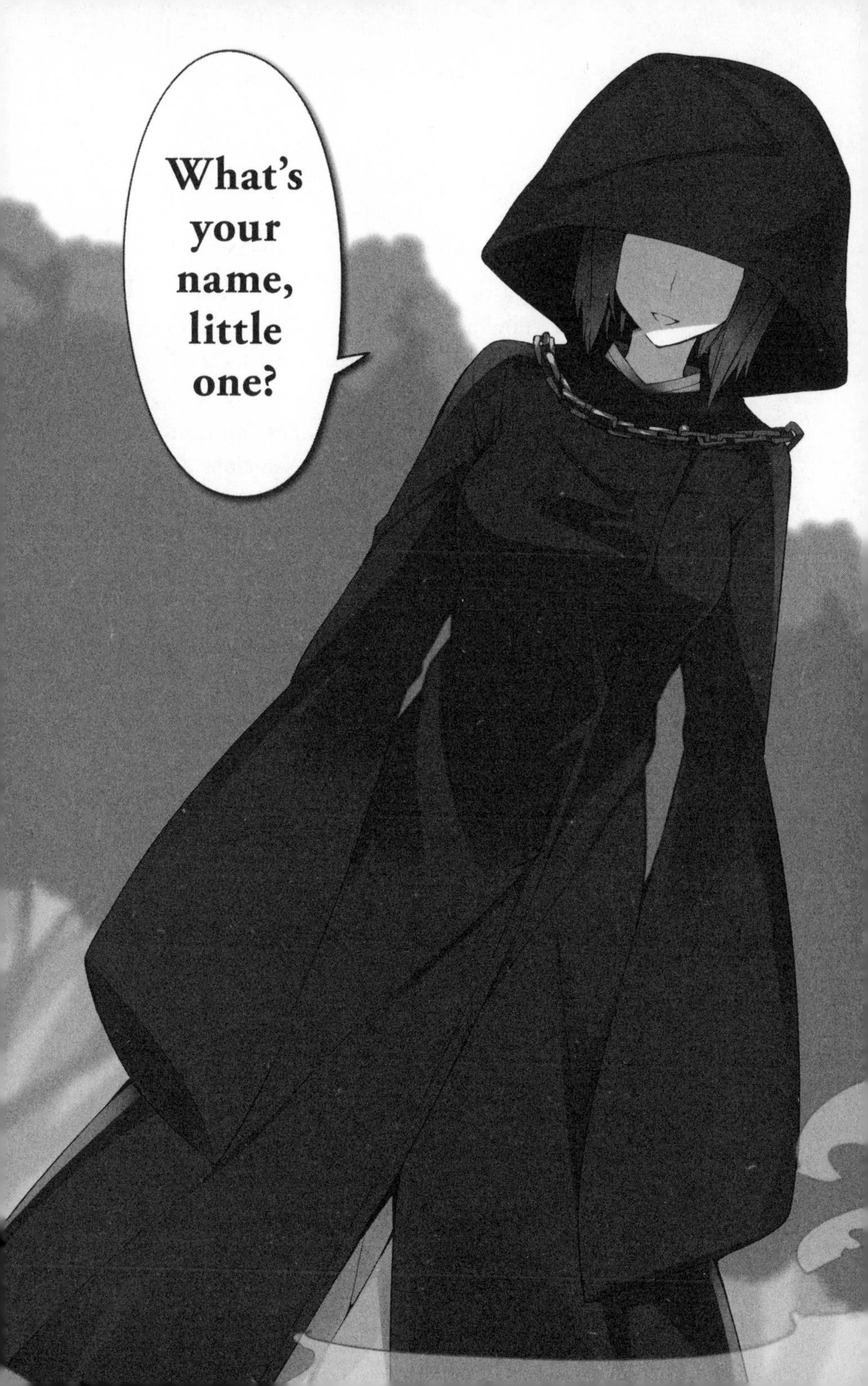
What's your name, little one?

....

There was a moment of silence, then the woman asked uncertainly, "...Is that a nickname?"

"No, it's my real name."

She went quiet again, then finally seemed to compose herself. "*Ahem*, so you want to know how you can be like me? Let's see... Eat lots, study hard, and if you can become a great wizard, then I'm sure..."

If I could become a great wizard, I could get a huge rack.

Being a top spell-caster was the path to an abundant endowment!

"Yes... If you can become a great wizard, I'm sure one day, you'll be able to use that spell. But I can't say I really recommend it." The hooded woman kept talking, but I didn't hear her. My head was already full of thoughts about becoming a great wizard.

"Anyhow..." I was still muttering "great wizard, great wizard" as the woman put her hand on my head and looked around. "Say, little one. Are you by yourself? Aren't there any grown-ups around? I'm sure there must have been somebody who broke the seal of this grave... I see the pieces of it right there, and I'm sure it didn't break itself..."

The woman cocked her head in confusion and started collecting the bits of my toy that were scattered at her feet.

"I wonder who freed me. They can't possibly have gone far... Well, I guess you wouldn't know anyway."

Then the woman walked to the middle of the crater she'd created with her spell. The big, black monster was lying there, just about breathing its last.

The hooded woman placed her hand on its head...

"Sleep just a little longer, O other half of mine," she whispered. "This world is yet too peaceful for you to awaken..." Then her hand glowed as if she was absorbing something from the beast. Before my very eyes, the giant creature shrank down and down. It shrank until it was the size of a kitten, and then it kept shrinking until it disappeared.

"All right, then. In that case, I'd better... Hmm? What are you doing, little one?"

The hooded woman looked at me. I was collecting the pieces of my toy from the ground.

"I'm picking up my toy. Our family is poor, and this is the only thing I have to play with."

"Wha—? No, look, that's not a toy, okay? Its job is to seal up a scaaary Dark God. Those pieces are important...... Wait, what?"

I quickly put the pieces of my puzzle back together and immediately realized some of them were missing. Three of them, to be exact.

"Three of the pieces went somewhere because of your spell, miss. Will you help me look for them?"

"No, no way! This makes no sense! There's no way you could put the pieces together so easily! Even sages have failed to break that seal, so how...?" The woman had her chin in her hand, looking troubled. "Listen, little one. How long have you been on these sealed lands? Didn't the village grown-ups tell you to stay away from here?"

"My mom said that whenever people tell you to *Stay away* or *There's nothing here* or *Better keep out*, it almost always means there's treasure, so I've been coming here every day."

"Wh-what are you saying...?!" The woman's voice went up an octave, and her face contorted. Finally, she came up beside me and planted her hand firmly on my head. "I can't say this makes much sense, but it looks like I'm the one who needs to thank you, little girl. Is there anything you want? I know I don't look like much, but I'm a mysterious wizard with tremendous powers. I'd like to grant a wish for you before I go."

"A wish?"

"That's right. Whatever you want, okay? Anything at all..."

"World conquest."

"...S-sorry, that's not really feasible. I wonder what's going on here. This girl might be something bigger than she appears. Er, do you have a different wish?"

I could just make out her eyes under her hood, and I could see she was frowning a little.

"Okay, then give me big boobs."

"Th-that's not really possible, either. J-just how old are you anyway, sweetheart? I think you're a little young to be worrying about that sort of thing."

Another dead end. All right, then…

"Make me the Demon King."

"L-look, I'm sorry, okay? Let me amend what I said. Compared to someone as impressive as you, I don't really have that much power, so I can't grant wishes as big as yours." I saw a bead of sweat run down the hooded woman's cheek.

I held up the pieces in my hands. "…Okay, well, my toy is missing three pieces. Just help me look for them."

"Wait! Now, that's thinking too small—I *can* do better than that! B-besides, you shouldn't play with those shards! That beast from earlier—I've only sealed her away again, you understand?! Don't ever come back here, okay?! Come on—isn't there something? Wish for something just a little bigger…!"

The woman crouched down to look into my eyes, genuinely upset now.

…Something a little bigger. A little bigger…

Okay—

"Teach me that spell you did."

Chapter 1

Wizards with Crimson Eyes

1

It was just an average morning for me. Our homeroom teacher was calling roll.

"Take your seats, please… Arue! Kaikai! Sakiberii!"

Each student answered to her name. All of them were girls. In our school, girls and boys were in different classes.

We were a small class, just eleven students, so my name came up quickly.

"Megumin!"

"Present."

When my name, the last on the list, had been called, the teacher nodded in satisfaction. "Good, good, looks like everyone's here. All right, then…"

"T-Teacher!"

He was about to put away the roll, but the girl next to me raised her hand, looking like she might cry.

"My name hasn't been called…"

"Hmm? Oh, sorry! I forgot there was one person on the next page. Sorry about that! *Ahem*… Yunyun!"

"P-present!"

Yunyun, whose longish hair was tied back with a ribbon and who gave off a definite overachiever vibe, blushed a little as she answered.

Ours was a small school in the hamlet known as Crimson Magic Village.

When they reach the right age, children of our village come to the school to receive a general education, and when they turn twelve, they start studying magic under the tutelage of a so-called Arch-wizard, an advanced class of wizard.

Members of the Crimson Magic Clan are born with exceptionally high intelligence and magical ability, and typically they study in school until they learn their magic. In other words, around here, acquiring magic is equivalent to graduating.

Which is another way of saying that no one in our classroom could use magic. The students in our class spent all their effort acquiring "skill points" so they could learn the spells they wanted.

The number of skill points one needed varied depending on what magic one wanted to learn. Stronger magic demanded more points.

But there was only one thing the girls in this class wanted to learn.

Advanced Magic.

This was a skill that allowed the wielder to employ a variety of powerful spells—enough to catch the attention of any young wizard. In our village, learning the Advanced Magic skill was tantamount to becoming a full-fledged adult. But...

"Okay, it's time for the test results. The top three scorers will receive a skill-up potion as usual. Come to the front of the class to get it. Starting with number three! Arue!"

I gazed out the window, sparing only a glance at our phlegmatic classmate as she stood to receive her potion.

"Number two, Yunyun! Well done—that's what I expect from the daughter of our chief! Keep up the good work."

"Oh, y-yes, sir!"

I glanced over and saw Yunyun getting up from her desk, her face bright red.

There were only two ways to gain skill points: raise your level by defeating monsters and gaining experience or consume a skill-up potion. Those potions were very rare, though, so students eager to attain Advanced Magic fought hard to get them.

"Finally, number one, Megumin!"

I stood to get my potion when my name was called. Yunyun was looking at me ruefully.

"Excellent score, as ever!" the teacher said to me. "I have to think you've got enough skill points to learn Advanced Magic any day now, though... Well anyway, keep raising the bar!"

I went back to my chair with my potion and resumed staring out the window. From our classroom on the second floor, I had an excellent view of the village.

I wondered if that person I met when I was so young, whose name I'd never even gotten to ask, was doing well somewhere out there in that big, wide world.

While the teacher was busy exhorting the other students to study, I pulled a card out from close to my chest. It was called an Adventurer's Card. The JOB field was filled in with the word ARCH-WIZARD.

LEVEL: 1.

Below that, it showed I had forty-five skill points. And in the field showing skills I could learn, glowing letters indicated that learning Advanced Magic would require thirty points.

"The rest of you could learn a thing or two from Megumin. Work hard so you can get that Advanced Magic as soon as possible! All right, time for class!"

I let the teacher's voice go in one ear and out the other as I gazed at something else in the SKILLS field of my card... Displayed in grayed-out letters was the word EXPLOSION, with a skill-point value of fifty. I ran my finger over it.

In the Crimson Magic Clan, learning Advanced Magic made you

an adult, but that wasn't the spell I was after. Even now, the words that robed woman had intoned, that spell of ultimate destruction, were burned into my mind.

I was going to acquire Explosion.

And then one day, I was going to show that woman what I had learned...

2

During the break after first period, a hand came slamming down on my desk.

"Megumin! You know why I've come!"

The speaker was Yunyun, who sat next to me. She was the daughter of the chief of the Crimson Magic Clan and an excellent student in every subject.

"Yes, yes. Incidentally, what *is* my breakfast going to be today? I'm famished."

"O-oh really? Well, for a side dish today, I really worked hard to make— W-wait, no! Why do you assume I'm going to lose?! T-today I'm going to win! Today is the day I, the daughter of the chief, achieve victory!"

She was also my self-proclaimed rival and the one who made my meals every day.

Despite her declaration, Yunyun put her boxed meal on my desk. As for me, I set down the potion I'd earned earlier.

"All right, then I shall determine the nature of our duel, as always. Surely, I can be granted a little handicap against the chief's daughter. And I hardly think a packed meal against a rare and valuable potion would normally be considered a fair wager."

"Y-yeah, I know that. Just go ahead and name the terms!"

What a soft touch.

"Very well. Our duel will consist of who, at the next physical measurement, shall prove to be more compact and thus friendlier to the environment."

"That's no fair! There's no way I can beat you at that!"

What...?!

"I know I'm the one who suggested this, but your bragging is really getting on my nerves! We are the same age, so there can hardly be that much difference between us! This young woman's ego is way too big!"

"Ow, that hurts! Stop it! I thought we were competing at the measurements! If you're that worked up about it, why not have a contest in gym class?!"

As I bopped Yunyun repeatedly, the other girls all filed toward the nurse's office.

It was all right: As I grew up, I'd investigated what I'd been told as a child, that becoming a great wizard would also mean a great rack, and it seemed to be more than just talk. Maybe an intense magical cycle improves blood flow and encourages growth or something, because an inordinate number of the best wizards in the village were exceptionally well-endowed.

As the top student in my class, I expected the day would soon come when I joined the ranks of those alluring Arch-wizards. The thought filled my mind as I headed for the nurse's office, Yunyun following frantically behind.

"Hey, Megumin! If you're so sure, how about just a contest of who's taller? No, hey, don't leave me behind...!"

The physicals had already started when we got to the nurse's office.

I was the smallest in my class full of girls. I had my suspicions, however, that the problem was nutritional in nature. Thanks to my father, a magical-item craftsman with unique tastes, my family was always destitute. Our collective diet left much to be desired, and I thought it might be stunting my growth.

"Ah, Arue, you've grown again. Maybe more than anyone in class. All right, next is...Megumin... *Ahem*, as I tell you every time, standing on your tiptoes and puffing out your chest doesn't make any difference, all right? I'm using measurement magic, so holding in a big, deep breath isn't going to change the numbers."

My modicum of resistance went in vain as the nurse used her magic to figure out my measurements.

"Good… Hmm, you haven't grown much, Megumin. Well, anyway. Next, Yunyun."

"Oh, no, I'm sure I grew… I'm gonna lose… Awww, I knew it! I lost to Megumin again… Ow, ouch! Wh-why are you doing that?! You already beat me and took my food—why do you have to hit me, too?!"

"Ask that disgustingly well-developed chest of yours!"

"M-Megumin, stress stunts your growth!"

3

I was eating the breakfast that I had relieved Yunyun of.

"Megumin! Here's an expensive, organic, Neroid-infused pudding that's perfect for dessert!"

"Thank you very much. Hey, there's no spoon."

"Oh, s-sorry, just a second."

I was sitting in my seat, calmly eating Yunyun's packed meal and watching her scramble for a utensil. Suddenly, though, the pudding and the spoon were both slammed down on my desk.

"What's wrong with me?! I should be saying, 'Let's have a contest with the pudding as the wager!' Why am I always so eager to do anything you say, Megumin?!"

"Every day, Yunyun, I feel as if I am your dog or your cat, a pet you care for. So perhaps I could see fit to let you come home with me sometime soon. And we could stop off for something to eat on the way."

"What?! R-really…? No, steady, Yunyun! We're rivals, remember?! A-and anyway, don't talk to me about getting 'something to eat' when I know you just want to poach whatever I get!"

I wondered when exactly we had become rivals.

In any event, I gave the empty lunch box back to Yunyun. "That was quite tasty, thank you. I appreciated the little flavor boosters you added today. They were excellent. Tomorrow, perhaps you could focus on protein."

"O-oh, is that what you want? Well, for tomorrow, I can…" In the middle of happily returning the lunch box to her bag, Yunyun stopped. "Wh-*what* is wrong with me?! Why do I always…?!"

"Take your seats! Time for class. You shouldn't be bringing pudding to school anyway. Consider it confiscated!"

""Oh no!""

We suddenly found our pudding in the hands of the teacher, who had arrived when we weren't looking.

Class started, notwithstanding Yunyun, who was moping "My pudding…" from the seat beside me.

The teacher wrote a hierarchy of magical spells on the blackboard and told us to copy it into our notebooks. As we copied silently, the teacher stood at the lectern and began to talk about magic and also to make a show of stuffing his face with our pudding.

"Okay. Today, I'm going to talk about a special branch of magic. First, consider the three written here. Basic magic, intermediate magic, and advanced magic. I assume I don't have to explain these. And I think you all believe that advanced magic is the most powerful magic available."

Then the teacher wrote three more names of spells on the board.

"In addition to advanced magic, however, specialized branches of magic exist, including blasting magic, detonation magic, and explosion magic. These spells boast immense power, but on top of being difficult to learn, they're inefficient, and there aren't many opportunities to use them."

My attention, which had been focused entirely on the pudding in the teacher's hand, shifted at the mention of explosion magic.

"First, blasting magic. This is powerful enough to split boulders, and mages who learn it are frequently called upon to assist in national public works projects. However, it requires roughly as many skill points as advanced magic. I would avoid it unless you fancy a career in civil engineering."

Blasting magic. Blasting magic...

I was careful to make a note of it in my notebook, pricking up my ears to be sure I didn't miss a word of what the teacher said.

"Next, detonation magic. This was the special magic of a legendary Arch-wizard. Every monster that faced her was buried by her series of detonation spells. However, every use of this spell requires an extraordinary amount of MP. The average mage would be completely exhausted trying to launch several of them in a row. Even if you've got confidence in your MP, learning detonation magic isn't very practical."

Detonation magic— Detonation magic—

I quickly wrote *detonation magic* in my notebook.

Then the instructor set down his chalk and resumed stuffing the last of the pudding into his face.

Grrr... Right when he was about to get to the most important of all, explosion magic.

"Teacher. About the last one—explosion magic..." I raised my hand and rose from my seat. All my classmates turned to look at me.

Our teacher just laughed. "Forget about explosion magic. The number of skill points you'd need is absurd, and if you finally did learn it, you'd discover it takes so much MP that even users with abundant magical power often can't get off a single shot. And if by chance you *were* able to use it, well, it's so powerful, you'd not only take out the monsters you were targeting but probably alter the surrounding landscape, too. If you tried to use it in a dungeon, you'd bring the whole thing down on your head, not to mention attract every monster in the area with the noise. Listen to your teacher, kids: **Explosion magic is just a gimmick.**"

4

Third period. Language class.

"Okay, everyone. Grammar and language are very important to us Crimson Magic Clan members. Why would that be? ...Megumin! Tell me why those things are so important to our people."

I stood up when the teacher called on me. "Because quick incantation and correct pronunciation affect your ability to control your magic."

"Three points out of a hundred. That'll never do."

"Th-three?!"

How could I, of all people, get just three points...?! Three points...

I sat back unsteadily in my chair, while the teacher moved on to Yunyun.

"Yunyun, you're next! Maybe you can give me the right answer."

"Y-yes, sir! Some of the magic used in creating ancient seals makes use of old systems of writing. In order to understand these so-called magic formulas, it's essential to study the relevant languages."

"Thirty points! I appreciate your drawing on concepts like seals and magic formulas, but the rest comes up short!"

"Thirty points?! ...Thirty points..."

Yunyun sat down, disheartened, while the teacher sighed as if to emphasize how disappointed he was in us.

"*Sigh...* Are these really my top students...?"

""Ouch!"" Yunyun and I exclaimed, but the frustrated teacher ignored us, pointing to another student.

"Arue! Why are the fundamentals of grammar and language so important to the Crimson Magic Clan?"

Arue, the third most distinguished student in class, stood at her desk and puffed out her chest. "**In order to avoid weird nicknames**, such as Fire-Breathing Fire-User. In addition, so that your prebattle speech can **make the battlefield a place of passion and drama**."

"One hundred points! Yes, nicknames are very important to us Crimson Magic Clan folk. I myself have the greatest among the nicknames in this village. And of course, each of you is going to have to come up with a nickname when you graduate. Right, next is gym class. I'll show you some examples!"

5

The school's courtyard was such in name only; in fact, it was simply a barren patch in front of the building where the grass had been burned away using fire magic. Our teacher stood there wearing a cape, letting something burn for some time.

The smoke from the smoldering something had been rising for a while, so one presumed our teacher had been here quite early in the morning getting ready. Most likely, the burning thing was an expensive rain charm the teacher had purchased to summon clouds just for this class.

Our teacher nodded once, apparently satisfied by the size of the clouds gathering overhead.

"All right! Time for gym class–cum–battle training! Now, what is the most important thing to us Crimson Magickers in battle? Let's see… Yunyun! You tell me!"

"M-me?! Er, uh, in battle, what matters is…b-being calm! You need to be totally unmoved no matter what happens!"

"Five points out of a hundred! Next, Megumin!"

"Five points?!"

Yunyun kept muttering "Five points…" as the teacher moved on to me.

The most important thing in battle? There could be only one answer to that!

"It's destructive force, sir. The ability to trample everything in one's path! Strength—that is what's most important!"

"Fifty points! Yes, strength is important. A real Crimson Magic battle can't get going without sufficient destructive force. But you're still wrong! That's why you're missing half the score!"

"H-how could I—I, of all people—get just fifty points…?!"

"Me, I only got five…"

"Pfeh!" Our teacher spat on the ground as if to say, *These are my best students? I'm disappointed.*

""Oh!"" Yunyun and I exclaimed, but our nasty teacher ignored us and pointed at another student.

"Arue! I'm betting you know the answer to this! You, with that fantastic eye patch covering your left eye, must understand what's most important in battle!"

Our classmate, the one with the eye patch, the one who was rumored to look incredible naked, the one who hardly seemed to be the same age as the rest of us, took a step forward.

She pulled her eye patch up with a little tug and said, **"It's coolness, sir."**

"One hundred points! Excellent, Arue—have a skill-up potion! Yes, coolness is the answer! We Crimson Magic Clan members are showstoppers or we are nothing! Now, I'll give you a little taste of what I'm talking about… *Call of Thunderstorm*!"

The teacher intoned a spell of some kind, and blue-white lightning began to flash amid the clouds hanging above. It must have been some spell, because an unnatural wind began to whip around us. We tried to keep our hair from getting into our faces as our teacher thrust out a staff he had ready and raised it to the sky.

"My name is Pucchin! Arch-wizard and wielder of advanced magic…"

As he spoke, a bolt of lightning came crashing down to meet his upraised staff. He gave a flourish of his cape, letting the wind whip it behind him.

"Greatest homeroom teacher of the Crimson Magic Clan and he who shall one day occupy the principal's seat…!"

There was a roll of thunder and another lightning bolt. Our teacher froze, standing illuminated by the blue-white flash with his cape billowing behind him.

""""S-so cool!"""" our classmates chorused; when I looked over, I saw that only Yunyun wasn't part of the cheer, standing with her reddened face in her hands, quaking slightly.

I thought perhaps she was so overwhelmed by our teacher's awesomeness that she was unable to look at him, but then I heard her mutter, "S-so embarrassing…!"

Apparently, the rumors that she had most unusual sensibilities were true. I had heard tell of a mysterious condition where those in their adolescence become obsessed with the strangest things, and perhaps Yunyun was among those so afflicted.

The wind kept blowing as our teacher started moving again, clapping his hands and saying, "All right! Pair up with whomever you want! Then practice introducing yourselves to each other in a cool way, and try to work out an awesome pose, too!"

Yunyun flinched at that. I wondered what was wrong with her—and then I watched her look hesitantly around the courtyard before finally glancing in my direction. No doubt she wanted to pair up with me, but since she had proclaimed herself my rival, she couldn't bring herself to ask.

…How very annoying.

I was just thinking I would force her to pair up with me, then intimidate her to tears with my incredibly cool pose, when someone called to me.

"Megumin, do you have a partner? Want to work with me?"

I turned and saw, first and foremost, a pair of boobs coming toward me that I would never have imagined belonged to a girl who was twelve years old, just like me.

…How very, very annoying.

I heard a little "Oh…" from behind me. I didn't have to look to know it was Yunyun.

My eye-patched classmate, Arue, was the one who had called to me. She was stretching her neck and doing little jumps; maybe she thought she was warming up. In time with her bouncing, her chest…

……………… *This girl is my enemy!*

"Very well," I said. "According to my statistical study, you have a high chance of becoming a great wizard in the future. So let us settle here and now which of us is better!"

"C-can you figure out that sort of thing with statistics?!" Yunyun exclaimed, totally taken in, but I paid her no mind; I could not be bothered.

Our teacher bellowed, "Good, good. Everyone have their partners? If anyone's by themselves, they can work with me."

"What? Oh!" Yunyun looked around quickly, and when she realized she was the only one without a partner, her shoulders slumped, and she began trudging toward the teacher.

…………

"Arue. I'm afraid I'm not quite feeling well today, so I think I may ask to get excused from gym class. Maybe there was something bad in the food Yunyun gave me earlier."

"What?!" Yunyun exclaimed, an expression of sincere shock on her face.

"Teacher, I'm afraid I'm not feeling well. May I skip gym today?"

"What, again? I can't let you do that; you've never even finished an entire gym period. And this one's especially important. I won't stand for any malingering."

Seeing that the teacher wasn't inclined to be flexible, I started groaning and curled up on the ground.

"I hate to tell you this, but that won't work on—"

"I-it's awakening…! If this keeps up, the being inside me will take control of my body and…!"

"Hey, Megumin, you…! Don't tell me that thing sealed up inside you is trying to awaken…! Fine, no choice. Go to the nurse's office. Make sure she touches up your seal."

"Understood, sir. I'll show myself out."

"All right! Has everyone got a partner? Get started, then!"

I could hear the teacher behind me as I headed for the nurse's office.

It would be such a waste to burn up the hard-won calories from Yunyun's breakfast just for some gym class.

I got a legendary (and commercially available) nutrient drink from the nurse to keep up the power of my seal, then flopped down on a cot.

In the quiet room, I pulled the sheets up to my neck, then lay there thinking about what our teacher had said.

"Explosion magic is just a gimmick."

I pulled the sheets up even farther, over my head, and pretended I was asleep.

"T-Teacher! It's raining! It's... It's pouring! Teacher, we've seen how cool you are now; can't you stop this dumb storm?!"

"It's washing away the principal's prized tulips!"

"Oh— Oh no! I forgot, today is the day when the moon, the source of magical power, is at its fullest...! All the magical strength I'd been holding back came pouring forth without my meaning it to...! I'll do something about this storm! The rest of you, forget about me. Evacuate into the school!"

"Teacherrrr! Just admit that you were only thinking about your performance, not how to stop the spell!"

My eyes drifted shut to the sounds of shouting from the courtyard.

6

"Let me ask you something, Megumin. Why are you parading around in front of my seat, making a big deal about your skill-up potion? Is there something you're trying to tell me?"

"Nothing in particular… But I must say, Yunyun, your lunch looks delicious today."

"Y-you think so? I made a second lunch, other than the one you'll take from me… A-and I'm not giving it to you! I have a lunch to use for wagers already, and if you take this one from me, I won't have anything to eat, so I'm not getting into any contests over it!"

"…"

"Stop it. Don't just swirl that potion in front of me. Hurry up and drink it!"

"……"

"I—I said, stop it! I swear, I'm not giving this to you! N-not even if you give me those puppy dog eyes………… I-I'll only…give you half………"

I was munching on Yunyun's lunch when an announcement sounded through the school building.

"The mysterious storm that came through this morning has been adjudged by Mr. Pucchin to be unquestionably the work of the Dark God sealed away in the corner of our village. The principal investigated as well and found clear evidence of the presence of magical power, indicating that the storm was artificially created. As all faculty will be required to help control the rain, afternoon classes are canceled. Going home will be dangerous on account of high winds, lightning, and intense rainfall, so students are instructed to remain at school and do self-study."

So our teacher had elected to blame this on the Dark God.

Just as I was trying to decide how to turn this into a way to convince him to treat me to dinner, several students stood up. It looked like they were going to the school library to kill some time.

Me, I had something I wanted to learn, too.

I shoveled the rest of the lunch I'd gotten from Yunyun into my mouth…

"H-half! I said I'd give you half!" she exclaimed as I returned the lunch box to her and followed the others to the library.

* * *

There are a great many books in our school's library, as one might expect of a place that produces as many magic-users as Crimson Magic Village. We have everything from fairy tales of dubious veracity to how-to books that serve no discernible purpose.

Yunyun, who had decided to tag along without my permission, was going through the shelf of how-to manuals, searching for something.

The Big Book of Forbidden Magical Spells for Making Friends Instantly.

How Even a Snail Can Learn to Get Along.

I didn't know why she had picked those particular books, but I saw the way her eyes sparkled as she read them, so I decided to just leave her alone. Instead, I ran my finger along the other books, looking for one in particular.

Secret Tales of the Birth of the Crimson Magic Clan.

The Fall of the Country of Magical Technology.

The Dukes of Hell, Vol. 4: The All-Seeing Demon.

Rumors Revealed: The Truth About Alternate-World Dwellers Among Us.

I passed over all the dumb and obviously irrelevant books until I found the one I was searching for.

The Effectiveness of Explosion.

I picked up the book and flipped the pages.

Explosion magic boasts the greatest destructive power of any spell and is the ultimate offensive magic, capable of dealing damage to any entity or object. The exact method of learning Explosion has not come down to us in full, now being known only to those who have spent long periods of time researching magic or to nonhuman magic-users of tremendous age.

My finger stopped there.

…I wondered who or what it was I had seen using this spell.

Further, because of the excessive difficulty of learning Explosion weighed against its limited usefulness, mages who acquire this spell are referred to as "pitfall wizards" and are frequently rejected when they offer to join adventuring parties.

That caused my devotion to explosion magic to waver just a little.

When I was a child, I had seen Explosion devastate all before it. Ever since then, I had been completely mesmerized by the spell and the person in that hood, but...

It is simply impossible for magic-users of average intelligence to learn the spell at all, and the immense MP required means that even those who learn the spell are sometimes unable to use it. Why a spell like this was developed at all remains a mystery; currently, it is learned only by non-human spell-casters who have lived so long that they have enough skill points lying around to learn the spell on a whim.........

...I decided not to read any more and put the book back on the shelf. I thought it might break me to keep going.

Beside the Explosion book, another title caught my eye.

The Unfettered Lord.

Drawn by the unusual name, I picked up the book.

It turned out to be the story of an elderly, demented former ruler who dragged his two nurses along as he wandered around, trying to set the world to rights. Some little thing gave away that the old man was a lord, whereupon a handful of villagers came to him to complain about an evil ruler, and the evil ruler tried to convince him that, no, the villagers were lying.

The old man declared that it takes two to argue and launched himself at both the villagers *and* the evil ruler, who banded together to fight him off. The old man insisted that he was going to burn the place to the ground, whereupon his nurses calmed him down by telling him it was time for dinner.

The villagers and the evil ruler, having fought on the same side together, discovered how wondrous it was to work with each other, and at last they built a metropolis to rival any city anywhere...

...I wonder where Volume 2 is.

As I was looking for more of the story, though, I overheard some very un-library-like talk.

"Hang on—what have you got there? Whoa, ugh! What, don't you have *any* friends?"

I looked over and saw one of our classmates with Yunyun.

This… This development called for…!

"F-friends… Well, I…"

"…Really don't have any, right? Otherwise, why would you be reading……*Fish Are Friends…*? Sh-sheesh. Put this thing down. At least stick to mammals…"

"That is quite enough!" I exclaimed, jumping out in front of them and pointing a finger at our classmate. "You are pathetic, teasing a young girl in pain! And later you will take advantage of that same wounded heart by pretending to be her friend and making all sorts of outrageous demands of her! Others you may deceive, but my eyes will not be blinded!"

"What?!" It was obvious how deeply shaken our classmate was that I had seen through her plans so easily. "H-hold on—I swear I don't know what you're talking about! I just thought Yunyun's book looked interesting…"

"M-Megumin, what's wrong with you? Have you been reading some weird book that's been giving you ideas? She—she was just talking to me…"

I ignored the excuses of Yunyun and our classmate. "No, I simply scented trouble, and since I had some time to kill, I decided to butt in. Also, considering that I cut class earlier, I was feeling bad being the only one who hadn't made a dramatic entrance."

""That's ridiculous!"" both girls shouted at me, and that was when the library door flew open.

"Hey, you kids, pipe down in here! Library voices! We somehow managed to stop the rain the Dark God sent. I guess the principal and I together are stronger than that evil spirit."

"Teacher, didn't you say something about your own power overflowing? I sort of feel bad for that god with you pinning everything on them," our classmate jibed, all too aware of the way our teacher's story kept changing.

"No, when the villagers went to check on the tomb of the Dark God, they found the seal actually was broken. Some idiot must have been playing with it. Several shards of the seal are missing. They tell me the god, or one of their servants, could have come popping out at any time. The seal targeted the Dark God, so it's less effective on their servants, who might be able to slip past it. Until they finish the resealing, you should make sure to go home in groups."

Such was what the teacher told us.

7

"Hey, have you heard? It was seven years ago. Back when we were kids, there was another time the Dark God's seal almost broke, or so they say. You know that big crater in front of the tomb? That's supposed to be from when a wandering wizard sealed up the Dark God."

The story seemed to be on all my classmates' lips when I got back to the classroom. Even in a rustic area like this, people loved to share weird rumors.

I had been young enough that I didn't remember the events too clearly, but I at least understood that this "wandering wizard" was the hooded person who had rescued me.

All the school's teachers had gone to have a look at the tomb, so apparently, we students were free to go home for the day. Our classmates filtered out, sticking close to other girls who lived near them, until only Yunyun and I were left in the classroom.

My house was on the very edge of Crimson Magic Village, so I didn't have any neighbors to go home with. Then again, another reason I'd been left behind might have had something to do with my tendency to spot classmates who were eating somewhere and edge up to them, saying, "Oh, hey, that looks awfully good."

I got out of my seat, resigned to going home alone.

"Oh…" Yunyun, left in the classroom like me, reached out a hand as if to stop me and made a little sound.

"What is it?"

"Oh! N-nothing, I just… I was just thinking, Megumin, your house is right on the way to my house, and…"

Yunyun's house was in fact the one belonging to the chief of the village, which stood smack in the middle of town. My house was hardly "on the way." In fact, it would mean a considerable detour…

"…Would you like to go home together?" I asked.

"Could we?! Oh, but with us being rivals, we shouldn't get too close…!"

Yunyun had looked so thrilled, but she immediately followed it up with some kind of obnoxious statement. I pattered out of the classroom, leaving her to follow me, almost in tears.

"Wait for me! T-tomorrow! Tomorrow we go back to being rivals, okay?!"

When Yunyun and I got outside, the sky was still heavy with clouds. Had our teacher really effected such a dramatic change in the weather just for his little show? Our teacher might be a worthless person in a great many ways, but I would give credit where credit was due: The willingness to burn an expensive talisman for the sake of one single instant was the mark of a first-class Crimson Magic Clansman.

I was walking assiduously homeward, Yunyun following behind, when she said, "S-say, Megumin. Do you have some time? I mean, uh, if you don't mind…"

Then she invited me to go have a little snack somewhere. Her treat, no less.

"I have, of course, no reason to refuse you. To what do I owe this curious turn of events?"

"Huh? Erm, I was just hungry..." Yunyun blushed as if she was downright embarrassed.

"Well, I suppose you are a growing girl, so it can't be helped. But I must wonder whether it's proper for a young woman to display such an appetite."

"Hold on a second! How can you of all people say that, Megumin?! For that matter, I'm hungry because *you* ate my lunch! A-and..." Yunyun's voice suddenly got smaller. "A-anyway, I thought getting something to eat with a friend, stopping off somewhere on the way home... It just... I thought it sounded...fun..."

"Hrm? What was that you said?" I deliberately turned my ear toward the muttering Yunyun. Red-faced, she insisted it was nothing, but I continued to harangue her about it until she repeated her words, even if she cried while she did it.

8

"G'day to you! Welcome to the greatest among the cafés of the Crimson Magic Clan—mine! Ah, if it isn't Megumin, Hyoizaburou's girl. I've heard how hard you're working at school. They say you're the greatest genius of the Crimson Magic Clan. A meal out's a special occasion for you. What'll ya have?"

"Something with plenty of calories that will keep me full for a long time, please."

"Megumin, that order isn't very ladylike! Erm, we'll have whatever you recommend today, sir..."

Yunyun and I were on the terrace of the only café in town. The owner, who apparently knew my father, gave us menus.

"My recommendation, eh? Today I think you should try the Dark-God-Blessed Stew or the Rock-Wurm Spicy Spaghetti."

"The spicy spaghetti, please."

"I'll have this Lambwich Offering to the Magical Deity, please."

"Sure thing! One Rock-Wurm Spicy Spaghetti and one Lambwich Offering to the Magical Deity! Coming right up!"

"You know, I'll have the spaghetti, please!" For some reason, Yunyun blushed and changed her order; meanwhile, I nursed the fruit water I'd requested.

"Say, Megumin. I know this is sudden, but can I ask you something?"

"What is it? Given that you have treated me to a meal, I will answer most any question. Are you curious about my weakness? Currently, my weakness is sweets. A dessert after my meal."

"That's not what I'm asking about! And what do you mean, weakness? You always eat enough for three people!"

"Do they not say that sweet things are the enemy of a fair maiden? But what *is* it that you wanted to ask me?"

Despite my encouragement, Yunyun hesitated a moment longer. Just looking at her, I'm afraid, made me want to tease the poor girl.

"Megumin, uh, do you…? Do you have a guy you like or anything?"

I jumped to my feet. "Yunyun, you've turned downright scandalous!"

Yunyun was practically weeping. "N-no, I haven't! Aren't friends supposed to talk about, you know, their love lives and things when they chat together?! I just wanted to have one of those conversations! I'm not secretly implying there's somebody *I* like or anything!"

Her words mollified me enough to get me to sit back down. "How do I put this? Yunyun, you've always seemed rather odd for the Crimson Magic Clan. I heard how in gym you were practically too embarrassed to even strike a properly dramatic pose."

"I—I am weird, aren't I?! Ever since I was little, I've never quite felt like I was really one of the people of this village…"

What I'd said seemed to upset Yunyun. I knew she was strange. Maybe this was the side of her that left her isolated in class.

"So what type of guy do you like, Yunyun?"

"Huh?!" She was completely shocked to have me turn the tables on her.

"Isn't this what you wanted? A little love chat? Incidentally, I want a self-reliant man with no debt. Someone who would never be fickle and never cheat on me. Someone who always looks onward and upward and isn't afraid to work hard every day to achieve his goals. Someone serious and loyal."

"Serious and loyal, huh? You have a surprisingly kind and thoughtful streak, Megumin, so I thought you might like exactly the opposite. Someone worthless who never— Ow, ow! I—I was just kidding! ...Me, I want someone studious and grown-up, someone who'll listen politely to me while I tell him about my day..."

It was a calm afternoon. My self-proclaimed rival and I passed it in a long, meandering conversation as we worked our way home.

9

"I'm back!"

"Welcome home, Sis!"

Upon my return home, I was greeted by an excited voice and a pattering of feet. This welcome came from my younger sister, Komekko, who had just turned five years old.

She was wearing a hand-me-down robe of mine, and the hem of the overlong outfit was muddy.

"Argh... I see you've gotten mud on the hem of your robe. I told you to watch the house while I was gone, but you've been out playing somewhere again, haven't you?"

"Yep! I chased off the guy from the newspaper place, and then I went out to play!"

"Oh-ho, notched up another victory today? That's my little sister."

"Uh-huh! When I said, *'I haven't had solid food in three daaays!'* he left me a meal ticket!" Komekko proudly showed me the fruits of her labors.

As I mussed her hair, Komekko noticed something. "Sis, you smell good."

"Ah, that's my little sister again. I've brought you a present. A Lambwich Offering to the Magical Deity! Now then, eat until your very stomach explodes!"

"Awesome! I feel like I've become the Demon King himself! Okay, we can save the dinner *I* caught for breakfast tomorrow!"

Komekko was thrilled with the sandwich gift, but I hadn't been expecting what she said.

…*The dinner she caught?*

Recalling the time Komekko had collected a bunch of cicadas and suggested we fry them up for food, I was a little concerned.

"Komekko, what's this dinner you speak of? What have you caught?"

"Wanna see? It's a brutal, pitch-black magical beast I brought down after a life-and-death struggle!"

And with that rather perplexing remark, she disappeared into the house.

Please don't let it be bugs. Please don't let it be bugs!

I could only wait and pray until Komekko returned, holding…

"Mrrrow…"

…what appeared to be an absolutely exhausted black kitten. What in the world had happened to it?

"…That's quite some prey you have there."

"Uh-huh. I really worked hard for it! She tried to fight me at first, but when I bit back, she saw things my way."

"I'm certainly glad you emerged victorious, but remember our conversation about not biting things at random?"

Komekko nodded seriously at me, and I took the kitten from her. The animal curled up into my chest; she must've been through something pretty awful.

Komekko grabbed my sandwich with both hands and took a huge bite, then regarded the half-eaten food critically before holding it out to me. "...Want some?"

"I am quite full, so you should eat all of it, Komekko. But may I keep this fuzz ball for the time being?"

"Sure!" Komekko happily set about the work of finishing the sandwich.

I let the cat loose in my room, where she curled up on my bed as if it belonged to her.

"Now then, I wonder what I'm going to do about you."

She was so brazen. Maybe she really was something bigger than I imagined.

I knew I couldn't let Komekko make breakfast out of her, but even so, we didn't have the resources at home to feed an extra mouth. If I just released her back into the wild, though, and Komekko found her again, she might really get eaten.

That left me with only one choice—

10

The classroom was humming.

"...Megumin? ...M-Megumin?"

"Good morning, Yunyun. Why the face?"

Yunyun offered me a good morning in return, her eyebrows still furrowed in an expression of concern.

"Do you have to ask? ...What's with...*that*?"

"My familiar."

The "that" to which Yunyun referred was the black cat lying on her back on my desk, playing with my finger.

I introduced her to the classroom.

"Familiar?! I thought only wizards in fairy tales had familiars!"

"Look at that adorable, shameless face! It's terrible! She's pretending to be a sweet little kitten, and all the while she'll be trying to get our lunches for her mistress, Megumin!"

"That's awful! But...okay, here's my food!"

The girls in my class were instantly smitten with my familiar. Maybe this kitten was a practitioner of attraction magic. If nothing else, she seemed to promise to reduce my food bills, and I certainly appreciated that.

"W-wow... She looks so soft...! Megumin, what's her name? Have you given her a name yet?" Yunyun asked. Her eyes sparkled as she went to pet the cat, but my familiar got up on her front legs threateningly as Yunyun's hand approached. She pulled her hand back, disappointed to realize even this tiny cat was rejecting her.

"I don't get it. Maybe she only likes you, Megumin?" Arue said, even as she reached out to pet the cat, who gladly accepted her ministrations, a sight that brought Yunyun to the edge of tears.

"I have not named her yet," I said. "As it stands, I'm concerned she would be in danger if I left her home by herself during the day, so I think I will bring her to school every day from now on."

The girls shared a collective worried look.

"She's so cute. I sure wouldn't mind, but I don't know what Teacher is going to say..."

"Yeah. She's adorable, but I don't think Teacher will let you. Even if she is really cute."

Hrm. I might have known our instructor would be a problem...

"Absolutely not."

That was the very first thing our teacher said when he walked in the room.

I held up the kitten, who was trying her very best to look as lovable as she could. "Teacher, this is my familiar. She needs my MP for sustenance. To separate us would be a death sentence for her."

"I said no. You can't even use magic yet; how can you have a familiar? Anyway, there are two things we don't allow at school: snacks and familiars! Now, go put her back where you found her."

So it was no use after all. In that case…!

"Teacher, this is another me. A fragment of my power resides within her. I was able to retain the majority of my strength, but this is, I promise you, also me. We are of one mind and one heart. We cannot be separated!"

"…This second you doesn't look very fond of being picked up."

"I am at a rebellious age, sir."

I let go of the cat, who scampered over to a wall in one corner of the classroom and began sharpening her claws on it.

"Now your 'fragment' seems to be instinctively sharpening her claws."

"That's because Crimson Magic Clan members must be ready for battle at any moment. I took most of the intelligence and rationality in our split, so my other self is like a beast with only brute strength and wild instinct…"

"Fine."

"Indeed, I know how sweet and lovable I look, but within— Um, did you say it was fine?"

The teacher had agreed so abruptly. Here I'd been ready to describe at length the life-and-death struggle over my very body that my "fragment" and I had waged.

"Yeah, I'm willing to see where this goes. I think it'll be funny."

That did not sound like a very teacherly reason, and frankly it gave me a sense of foreboding.

"No, Megumin! You have to go to the bathroom in your toilet spot! Here, over here! This is where you do pee pee! There, good! What a good girl, Megumin!"

"......"

"Won't Megumin's leftover food smell if we put it here? I think it should stay out of the sun."

"............"

"Oh! Bad Megumin! Didn't we say not to sharpen your claws there? You won't get away with this just by looking cute like that! You won't... Arrrgh, but you're just so cute, True Megumin!"

"Aaaaaarrrrrrgggghhhh!"

"Eek! False Megumin is on a rampage! Your true self finally made off with your intelligence and rationality, not to mention cuteness!"

Flipping over my desk only got me called False Megumin by one of my classmates.

"Who is false, I ask?! I am the True Megumin! Please stop using my name willy-nilly like that!"

"Wh-what are you so upset about, Megumin? Didn't you tell us that thing is a part of you? You said there was the intelligent and rational Megumin and the powerful and wild Megumin, right?"

"Megumin this, Megumin that, Megumin, Megumin, Megumin! I have reached my limit of hearing my name from every quarter! Please give her a name already!"

At my outburst, Yunyun, holding my fragment, said, "E-erm, but we've already been calling her Megumin all day today, and I think it kind of stuck... Look, Megumin even likes me now; she lets me pick her up! ...I think maybe this sweet little kitten should get to be Megumin, and *you* should be the one to change your— Ow, ow!"

"Traitor! Can you abide the name of your rival changing?! For that matter, I have heard the name Megumin more times today than in all the days since I started at this school!"

My classmates responded with drawn faces.

"I've kind of started to like the name Megumin for her..."

"Yeah... Our sweet Megumin, our cute Megumin..."

"Excuse me, but it sounds like you are trying to start something,"

I said. Being a member of the Crimson Magic Clan, one of whose pre-
cepts is always to accept a fight, I slid some chairs aside in preparation of
lunging at my classmates.

"...Norisuke," Arue said flatly. Apparently, she intended it to be a
potential name for my cat.

"...Perekichi," someone else volunteered.

"Choisaa."

"Marumo."

"Kazuma."

The cat in Yunyun's arms snorted in what might have been a sneeze
of disinterest at any of these names.

Yunyun, meanwhile, held up the animal. "She *is* a girl..."

"...Eh, Megumin's the perfect name, then."

"You're dead," I said, just about to jump at my antagonist, when
Yunyun interrupted loudly.

"Um... Ink! ...Er, I mean, m-maybe. Because, you know, she's a
black cat..."

"""""   """""
......

Silence descended upon the classroom... Until...

"Sure, that might be good. It's such a weird name, it'll be easy to
remember."

"What?! W-weird...?!"

...Hmm.

Yes, the name was odd, but that would help make it memorable.
What's more, the newly christened animal squinted in Yunyun's arms as
if to say, *Not bad.*

"Very well. For the time being, we shall go with this bizarre name
of Ink. If and when she becomes my familiar proper, I reserve the right
to give her a more awesome name, though."

"Bizarre?! Is that how you think of me?! Am *I* the weird one in this
village?!" Yunyun demanded, nearly in tears, as I retrieved Ink from her.

11

"Hey, Megumin. Want to go to the accessories shop today?"

We were on the way home from school.

I seemed to recall being told only yesterday that we weren't to be caught dead together, but for some reason, Yunyun was following me home again. Well, *I* didn't think of her as *my* rival, so it didn't matter to me.

"Accessories shop? Do we have one of those?"

"The smith started it as a hobby. Erm, um, M-Megumin…"

"Yes, yes, I'm sure it's always been your dream to stop and admire cute accessories with your friends on the way home from school. Let's go."

And so Yunyun and I headed for the blacksmith's place.

"Welcome, welcome! Well, if it isn't the chief's strange little daughter and strange Hyoizaburou's girl. What, what do you want? For a couple of young girls like you, I've got… Let's see… How about this giant great sword? I've got big axes and even a hammer, too."

"S-strange…"

"Why would you attempt to foist such brutal weapons upon two fair, retiring maidens? We do not need weapons anyway."

Personally, I blamed the blacksmith for setting up a weapons and armor shop in a town full of wizards. If he would at least make staves, he might get a few orders.

"Gigantic weapons are perfect for little girls to swing around. The contrast is the whole point! The defiance of expectations!"

"In what world would such girls ever exist? …Yunyun, what's wrong?"

Beside me, Yunyun was looking around the shop, her eyes goggling. "Um, I heard you started selling accessories as a side business…"

"Well, they're right there. Although they don't seem very popular in a village of people who only like uncommonly long swords and

needlessly complicated weaponry." The burly blacksmith gestured with
his chin at a corner of the shop. There, indeed, was a collection of accessories. If you considered knives to be accessories…

"I think when most people refer to 'accessories,' they don't mean
tiny weapons; they mean fashion items," I said.

"*Now* you tell me," the smith answered. "I never get any customers
in here, so I thought this might be a way to drum up some business."

Again, I felt his problems went back to a poor choice of location.
How was he even making a living?

"I know that look. You're wondering how I eat. I'm something of
an Arch-wizard myself. I use my magic to heat up my forge hotter than
anyone else to produce the best armor. I've got a certain reputation
among some armor nuts, y'hear? I can't name any names, but a young
lady from a certain noble family loves my product."

"Why would a young noblewoman love armor? Yunyun, I think it's
about time we—"

But Yunyun had picked up a silver dagger and was looking at it
admiringly.

"…Don't tell me you like it?"

Yunyun nodded emphatically.

Afterward, Yunyun and I parted ways, and I came home to be
greeted by Komekko, whose robe was once again muddy.

"Welcome home, Sis! What'd you bring me?"

"Nothing today, I'm afraid. But have you been outside again?
Apparently, the Dark God has nearly come unsealed in the village
recently, so be certain you're home before dark."

I couldn't tell how much of what I said registered with Komekko,
who was fidgeting and staring at Ink in my arms.

"*…Drool.*"

"?!" Ink scrambled up onto my shoulder, where Komekko couldn't
reach her. This cat had some nerve, clawing her way up her master's very
body like that.

"Sis, we're having meat for dinner tonight, aren't we?!"

I had some reservations as I looked at my little sister, who was perfectly happy to consume a handful of bugs or the beloved family pet. "Komekko, now, just wait a moment. Look how thin she is. There's hardly any meat there. Let us fatten her up first."

"Oooh. You're so smart, Sis!" She smiled innocently, and I wiped the mud from her face with a handkerchief.

"So what little games took you outside today, Komekko?"

"I found a toy, and I was playing with it! You wanna try it, too, Sis?"

...A toy?

The word nagged at me for some reason.

I seemed to remember I...

"Sis, let's take a bath! Kitty can come with us! It'll help cook the bitterness out!"

"Komekko, I can feel the fuzz ball on my shoulder quaking with fear. Please give her a break."

12

Komekko, Ink, and I shared a bath, after which I ate a simple meal and went to my room.

I heard a commotion from downstairs, presumably my mother getting home. My father was no doubt working on some weird magical device with such single-mindedness, he had forgotten to eat.

I lay on my thin bed mat, spread over the carpet, and rested Ink on my stomach.

Then I let the memories come to me.

"A toy. I think when I met that person, I asked her to help me find my toy," I murmured to myself, hugging Ink in the dark room, holding her up so she was right in front of my face. The cat was looking at me as if hanging on my every word. Her eyes were big and bold and lovable.

...Why?

Why did looking at her make me think of *that* person?

I pulled the covers up over my head, burrowing down into my bed like I always did.

"Hey, you've got some nerve for a freeloader," I said. But really, I enjoyed the feeling of Ink where she had curled up on my tummy under the covers.

I didn't expect to leave the village for a long time, not then.

I would go to school and look after my sister.

Just passing the days without anything changing. Or so I thought.

The Inscrutable Puzzle and the Dark God's Seal

I went to play where I always did, but there was something there today. Crouching in front of the tomb…

"It's a big ol' goblin!"

"…Hey, squirt. Don't confuse the great and magnificent yours truly with a measly goblin."

"I'm not a squirt; I'm Komekko."

"That right? …Yo, Komekko. What are you doing here anyway? Half of the great Dark God Wolbach is sealed in this tomb. Didn't your folks or anybody tell you to steer clear of this place?"

"Sure they did. But my big sis says members of the Crimson Magic Clan are duty bound to fight back against dumb rules."

"…O-oh. Well, that puts me in a bit of a tight spot, see. I really don't wanna have to silence a little squirt like you…"

The big, black not-goblin with the bat-like wings slumped his shoulders.

"I'm not a squirt; I'm Komekko," I reminded him. "And what are *you* doing here, Mr. Not-Goblin?"

"'Mr. Not-Goblin'… Here, squirt, take a good look! Check the monstrous horns! Scope the giant wings! I'm beefier than any goblin you'll ever see! I'm the right-hand man of the Dark God Wolbach, the high-level demon Lord Host! And don't you forget it!"

"Cooool!" I threw up my hands and cheered when Host spread his wings way open.

"Er, uh, well, look… I think you'll go far, kid. Usually I'd shut any witnesses right up, but I don't mind lettin' you off the hook. But you gotta do me a favor and not tell anyone about me. And everything we do here is a secret, okay? I'm treating you special, and you'd better appreciate it."

"Thank you very much," I said, not really understanding why. Then I sat down in front of Host and started poking at his big, tough foot.

"You're a weird one, squirt… Er, anyway, I'm busy with important stuff right now. Just keep out of my way, all right?"

Then he turned around and started doing something in front of the tomb… *Hey!*

"My puzzle!"

"Huh? It ain't yours; it's the key to breaking Lady Wolbach's seal… H-hey, hey, what're you—?!"

Host seemed upset about the way I was working on the puzzle.

"You're something else, kid! The great and magnificent yours truly's been sneaking into this village for months trying to solve that thing… All right, even I can finish it now! Here, gimme that!"

"Oh! No fair, Host!"

"Heh! All's fair for demons, kid. And show a little respect. It's *Lord* Host. Now we're gonna get Lady Wolbach back to full power. Then we can go on a nice rampage, just like we used to… Huh. This… This is weird…"

Host tried again and again to fit the pieces into the puzzle he'd taken from me, but he couldn't do it. Finally, his shoulders slumped again, and he glanced in my direction.

"…Yo, Komekko. I'll let you play with this puzzle. You wanna do the rest?"

"Nah, I'm too hungry now and I don't wanna. I'll let you do it, Lord Host."

"……Y'know, on second thought, how about we nix the 'Lord Host' business? I'll get you a little something to eat, so you wrap up this puzzle, Komekko."

"………"

"……Please, Lady Komekko?"

"Well, okay."

At that, Host spread his wings and started flapping away, although he didn't look very happy about it. I watched him go, then turned to the puzzle…

Lonely Masters
of the Crimson
Magic Clan

1

"Megumin! I'm sure you know we'll be having another contest today!"

It was a beautiful, clear day out, probably in response to the weather-control ritual a certain teacher had performed. When I arrived in the classroom, Yunyun was waiting for me. She seemed unusually upbeat today.

And then I realized why. Hanging at her hip was the dagger she had bought the day before.

She kept pointedly shifting it around so that it would be noticeable. How obnoxious. Was she hoping I would compliment her on it?

As I was not Yunyun's boyfriend or anything, I didn't intend to go out of my way to indulge her girlish whims.

"Very well, I accept. But since I have no skill-up potion to wager, what shall I offer if you win?"

"Your wager... W-well, okay, if I win, Megumin, you have to do any one thing I say..."

"Agreed. As a favor to you, I will even pick a form of contest that will be advantageous to you, Yunyun. The contest will involve that very cool dagger hanging at your hip. What do you say?"

"My dagger? Okay. I don't know what kind of contest you have in mind, but I'm game!"

When Yunyun, brimming with confidence, was seated at her desk, I put my hands down flat on the desktop. "Here are the rules: You attempt to stab that dagger in between my fingers, one after another. If you cannot reach ten—once in between each of my fingers—you lose. Simple, no?"

"Hold on! Just a second! There's no way I can do that!"

"It will be all right; I trust your skills, Yunyun. And if you do stab me, I will endure. Now, on your mark! One, two…"

"I give up! You win—again!"

Yep: just another average morning…

"…Phew! Well done. Another delicious meal."

"Awww… You could stand to do a normal contest *once* in a while…" Yunyun sniffled, taking back the empty lunch box I held out to her.

"…Come to think of it, Yunyun, how many more points do you need before you can learn Advanced Magic?"

"How many points? Another…three points. With three more points, I'll be able to learn Advanced Magic. And then… Well, I guess that'll mean graduating… Megumin, what about you?"

The Crimson Magic educational system was simple: When you learned a spell, any spell at all, you graduated.

I glanced at my Adventurer's Card and saw that the number of skill points it listed was forty-six. In the AVAILABLE SKILLS field, ADVANCED MAGIC was listed next to a glowing number thirty.

But the spell I wanted to learn was Explosion. And for that I needed…

"Another four points, it looks like. So I guess if things keep on like this, you will graduate before I do, Yunyun."

"What?! W-wait a second, Megumin. You always get better grades, so how can you have fewer points than I do? Wait—what?! Am I going to graduate alone…?!"

While Yunyun was still discombobulated, the teacher came in. The hubbub in the classroom fell quiet as he came to the lectern and prepared to call roll.

"All right, everyone, take your seats," he said, and then students answered as he read off their names. "…Dodonko! Funifura! Nerimaki!"

Our class was small, only eleven students, so my turn came around soon enough.

"Megumin! ……Oh, and Yunyun!"

"P-present! …Teacher, what was that pause before my name? Did you say 'Oh, and'? You were about to forget me again, weren't you?"

"All right, time for class! …Is, *ahem*, what I'd like to say. As a matter of fact, the monsters around the village have been unusually active lately. The principal has asked me to work with one of the village NEETs…er, I mean, a young person with time on their hands to hunt down the monsters, so you all can go home after lunch. Until then, study on your own in the library. Get to it!"

Then the teacher summarily left the classroom. Yunyun's eyes were still teary from having her question ignored.

This was Crimson Magic Village, a place even the Demon King's army feared. It was extremely unusual for monsters to be active around here. Normally they didn't even get near the village…

With those thoughts whirling in my mind, I wandered around the library looking for a book.

I wanted to find the sequel to the odd story I'd read the day before. *The Unfettered Lord, Vol. 2… The Unfettered Lord, Vol. 2…*

Ah, there it was.

"Yunyun, I have been looking for that book you're carrying. One of the several books you're carrying, actually, so if you aren't going to read it right away, may I read it first?"

Yunyun was carrying *The Unfettered Lord, Vol. 2* along with several other titles.

"Er… I don't mind, but, Megumin, do you even read books like this? Anyway, here." Then she passed me two different books: one titled

Goblins Can Make Small Talk, Too and another called *How to Make Friends and Influence Monsters.*

"Who asked for *these* books?! I meant *The Unfettered Lord!*"

"What? Megumin, you like this series, too?! Isn't it great? I've read it so many times! This is the second volume, *The Fake Ruler.* I can't believe the elderly councillor would go on a journey with two fake attendants; what an incredible twist...!"

"No spoilers! ...But I must question the choice of your other books. The titles alone sound awful. They're just...just too terrible..."

"Stop it, Megumin—what's with the pitying glance?! Here, look at this; it says even cacti have feelings! So we could be friends with plants...!"

...There was something wrong with this girl.

"My goodness. If you are so desperate for friends, then just retract your declaration of rivalhood with me, and..."

"Man, Yunyun. Are you reading that stuff again? If you want friends that badly, I'll be your friend. How about it?"

I turned toward the interruption and saw the same girl who had spoken to Yunyun earlier. It was our classmate...uh, our classmate...

"Well, if it isn't *Funikura*," I said. "Becoming a friend is not something one does *for* someone. It happens naturally."

"It's Funi*fura*! You could at least remember your classmates' names!"

Yunyun rushed up to the aggravated Funifura. "What was that? What did you say just now?!"

"Y-yikes! Yunyun, too close! I just said I would be your f-friend...!" Funifura had pulled back, afraid, as Yunyun looked at her with eager eyes.

Yunyun nodded several times, her face turning red. Ahhh! So Yunyun, the forever alone, was to have a friend at last! I had been somewhat worried for her future (not that it had anything to do with me), but now I could at last set my heart at ease...!

"I... I may not have much to offer, but I look forward to our friendship!"

"Uh, Yunyun, you do understand how friends work, don't you?! Or... Don't you?!"

...I could set my heart at ease...maybe...

2

"Come on, Yunyun! I'll give you a new one! It's just a rubber hair band. I can give you another! Look, Megumin feels bad about it, so just let it go!"

"But that... But that...! That was the first thing I ever got from a friend...!"

It turned out I could not set my heart at ease at all.

Funifura, it seemed, had given Yunyun a hair band with the advice to make herself a bit more fashionable. Yunyun was so happy to get it that she had gone back to the classroom and stashed it carefully in her desk.

And then...

"Why were you even looking through my desk anyway, Megumin?! Why would you shoot around and play with rubber bands?! What are you, a child?!"

I had tired of reading my book and had gone back to our classroom, where I'd passed the time shooting rubber bands out the window. Apparently, Yunyun's had been among them. Currently, her hair band was hanging from the highest branch of the tree outside the window, completely unreachable.

I was seated in a formal posture on the floor.

"You are misunderstanding. I could see a bagworm hanging on the branch outside the window. It bugged me more and more until I could no longer resist the urge to shoot it down, but because I failed to do so using the rubber bands in my desk, I just decided to borrow some more..."

"You didn't 'just' anything! What's a young girl even doing shooting rubber bands at a bug?! Arrrgh…!"

My head was bowed deeply; Yunyun could only sigh. "Dear Funifura, I'm so sorry! And after you went to all the trouble of giving that to me! I was planning to put it in a safe when I got home…!"

"Seriously, you don't have to do all that! That's going a little overboard! Anyway, hair bands are for using, not for…safe-ing!" Funifura seemed like she was discreetly drawing away from Yunyun. "Come on—it's almost lunchtime. Let's grab Dodonko and go eat."

It was the most casual of remarks.

"C-could we?! Eating lunch together… Why, it's like we're really friends!"

"That's because we *are* friends! Didn't we already cover that?"

It seemed Yunyun was still working off the hangover of being a loner for so long.

"That's a good idea. It is just the right time to have some lunch and then go home." I rose from where they had forced me into a formal sitting position on the floor, following them…

"…Megumin, did you even bring a lunch?" Yunyun asked.

"I did not."

"That won't do!" Funifura exclaimed.

…This was bad. I had just realized something terrible indeed.

I was perfectly happy for Yunyun having made some friends. But at the same time, a precious lifeline for poor indigent me had been cut off.

As Yunyun clutched her packed lunch and prepared to leave, I made a point of wandering around by her.

"Megumin, um… I might be able to spare just half my… Hey, no hugging! Don't worship me!"

They say three's a crowd, and when it's three young women, it's a very noisy one.

"I'm sure that guy is, like, totally into me! But I don't know what to do! I've got, like, this other guy, and in our past lives we swore to be together when we were reborn, right? So is this, y'know, cheating? I just don't know!"

"Aww, I think it's fine. Past lives are the past. This is now. Me, my destined one is a hot guy being held in the deepest depths of the darkest dungeon…at least, in my dreams. I mean, *anyway*, I'm pretty sure he is, so I can't wait to learn some magic and go rescue him."

This conversation was making me cringe.

"W-wow, you guys are amazing!" Yunyun, wearing a nervous smile, attempted to contribute.

We were sitting with our classmates Funifura and Dodonko, having lunch, but the discussion so far had been one unbroken stream of frankly mysterious talk of romance. It seemed they had started to confuse some love story they'd made up in their heads with reality.

"What about you, Yunyun? Who's your type…? Er, I mean, who were you with in your past life?" Dodonko asked, spearing some salad with her fork.

"Me?! Um, I'd like somebody quiet and mature, who'll nod along and listen while I talk about my day…"

"*Bo*ring."

"Yeah, no imagination."

"Well, I suppose that cannot be helped, Yunyun being so strange and all," I offered. "Incidentally, as I was a deity of destruction in my past life, I had no lover. Ah, thank you for the meal, by the way; that was delicious."

"Strange?! Hey, am I really strange?! Wait, Megumin, I said half! You ate it all!"

3

We were on the way home from school.

"I'm so glad you finally made a friend," I said to Yunyun, who was walking beside me. "You've been alone so long that I started to worry maybe you were a stinkbug in a past life, which would explain why nobody wanted to be friends with you even in this life. Truly, I was concerned."

"It's not like I enjoyed being by myself! …Gosh, Megumin, your mouth. There's some sauce here. A young lady like you could stand to pay *some* attention to your appearance, you know?" She dabbed at my mouth with her handkerchief in a very motherly way.

"I had been afraid that you would grow into a total naïf who could easily be taken in by some villainous man just because he claimed to be your friend, so I'm glad to know I need not worry so much now."

"Yeah? Well *I* worried that you might grow into someone totally helpless who could be taken in by some villainous man just because he said he would treat you to a meal, and I'm still worried."

My eyes met hers, and I jumped backward. "What an interesting thing to say. Do you take me to be so easy that I would just toddle off after any man who dangled some food in front of me?"

"You're the one who made fun of me first, Megumin. Or do you think *I'm* so easy that I would wander away with any guy who used the word *friend* on me?"

We stood there, facing each other down right in the road, each of us grinning weirdly at the other.

"I can just picture it," I said. "A young man comes along, croons, 'We're friends, aren't we?' and off you go!"

"Well, *I* can just picture *you* getting lost because you're so helpless and then breaking into tears and begging some guy who's totally the opposite of your type for food!"

…It was time to settle things with this self-proclaimed rival of mine!

I struck an intimidating pose; Yunyun took up a fighting stance, too, keeping a wary eye on me.

But at that most fraught of moments, someone called out to us.

"Well, if it isn't Megumin!"

I looked over and saw the cobbler's son from our neighborhood.

"Oh, Bukkororii. What brings you here?"

Bukkororii was something of an older brother to Komekko and me. He spent most of his time lolling around his house on the grounds that he was *"saving up my power until the day the world needs me."* It was most unusual to see him out-of-doors.

"I've heard the monsters are getting more active. Some of them are even coming close to the village. I've been around exterminating the beasts. They told me the day the world needs me has finally come, and I couldn't be more excited!"

Come to think of it, our teacher did say something about a village NEET hunting the monsters. Maybe the adults had just managed to score some free labor out of Bukkororii, but he seemed so happy about it that I decided not to say anything.

"I saw a really weird monster, too. I wonder what it was. Did we ever used to have something like that around here…?" In the middle of his muttering, Bukkororii suddenly caught Yunyun's eye. "**…My name is Bukkororii. Arch-wizard and wielder of advanced magic… First among the cobblers' sons of the Crimson Magic Clan and he who shall inherit the shoe shop…!** You're the chief's girl, aren't you? Nice to meet you."

"Oh! Uh, I-I'm Yunyun. Nice to meet you…" Yunyun blushed, evidently embarrassed by Bukkororii's overdramatic self-introduction; she looked at the ground and greeted him in a small voice.

What a waste of an excellent chance to introduce herself. I knew this girl was strange.

"So what are you two up to anyway? It kind of looks like you're having a battle."

"That's right! This young woman and I were about to engage in a blood-soaked duel to determine which of us is the greater! Now, Yunyun, have at it!"

"Wait! I thought we were just going to have a normal contest! I'm not ready for any blood-soaking!"

4

I opened the door of our ramshackle house and called out, "I'm hooome!"

Pattering footsteps came rushing through the hall and I was greeted with "Welcome back, Big Sis!"

Komekko came dashing into the entryway with a huge smile on her face. Her cheeks had mud on them, as did the hem of her robe. It looked like she had been off playing somewhere again.

"Komekko," I said, "I don't know where you've been, but I hear there are monsters coming right up to the borders of our village. I'm told some of them are especially bizarre. So don't go walking around by yourself too much, okay?"

"Uh-huh! I won't go walking around too much!"

"…Just stay inside until I tell you it's safe."

As I took off my shoes just inside the front door, Komekko handed me a piece of paper.

"…? What's this?"

"This really pretty but really pale lady came by earlier, and she said, 'Is there a renowned maker of magical items here?' and I said, 'No, there's no renowned maker of magical items here,' and so she said 'Oh, I see' and went away, but she left this piece of paper."

…?

On inspection, I saw that the paper was an order for a magical item. Next to the order itself was an inscription in stunningly beautiful handwriting: *I have been struck on many occasions by your most impressive items. It would be my pleasure to begin a good relationship with your shop…*

It went on to praise my father in rather fulsome terms.

…It was true; my father did make magical items for a living. But in spite of the powerful magic with which he imbued all his creations, every single one of them was a dud. Our visitor must have had him confused with someone else, even if I couldn't imagine who. And if not, then she had one twisted understanding of how business works.

"I'm sure it's a mistake or a prank," I told Komekko. "It looks like the shop's address is in Axel, that town with all the novice adventurers. Her name is…"

But before I could quite get to the end of the letter, Komekko tugged on the sleeve of my robe. "Sis, I'm hungry! Make some food! I brought the ingredients!"

"All right, all right, don't pull… I don't remember us having a lot of stuff to eat, though. Maybe there were some extra vegetables on hand?"

I allowed Komekko to drag me to the kitchen, where some spices and plates were already out, and there was even a stewpot standing ready. The limp remains of some vegetables sat beside it.

Well, it was no worse than an average dinner in our destitute household. Vegetable soup, then? But just as I was thinking that, I heard the pot rattle a little.

"…?"

When I opened the lid…

"…Er, Komekko, I think we should wait until she fattens up a little."

"She fattened! She's fatter today! When will we be able to eat her? Tomorrow?"

"Th-that's still a little early. Just be patient, okay?"

I'd made sure to give Komekko plenty of breakfast that morning, in hopes that our houseguest would be safe for the day. But clearly, I was going to have to start taking her to school.

Yes, that's what I'll do, I thought as I lifted the shaking Ink out of the pot.

5

There was no school today.

This accursed day came once every week, and it always tested me. Why? Well.........

"Mornin', Sis! You don't have school today, right? Let's have breakfast together, then!"

"...Komekko, our mother should have made breakfast before she left this morning. It must be in the kitchen. You can even eat my portion. I'm simply going to lie here motionless all day to conserve calories." I didn't move from under my blanket.

Komekko, however, didn't go away. "You can't get breakfast from Yunyun when you don't have school, right? Let's eat!"

...At that, I heaved myself out from under my blanket.

No school meant no Yunyun with her packed food for me to obtain. Normally I gave my breakfast here at home to Komekko, who seemed to be in a perpetual growth spurt, on the grounds that I could get breakfast at school. But on these days when I didn't have school, my sweetheart of a little sister invited me to eat with her.

"I can see you're right. So what's for breakfast today?"

"Rice balls with salmon!"

"...I guess that's about the best we can expect at the end of the month. I'm not much of a salmon person, though, so you can eat mine for me, Komekko."

"Let's feed it to her, then," Komekko said, spotting Ink as she crawled out from under the covers with me.

I knew how badly Komekko must want that salmon. My dear, sweet little sister. I patted her head and...

"...Drool."

...guided her into the kitchen, away from the drool-inducing sight of my cat.

"Here, Ink, you want the skin from my salmon, too?"

"Mrrrow!"

"The skin is full of nutrients," I said. "Be sure to eat it all."

After Komekko and I were done eating, I turned my thoughts to what I was going to do that day.

My father, as I've said, was a craftsman specializing in magical items, but unfortunately, all his creations had little quirks that made them unsalable. Even when he did manage to sell something, he always wound up bargained down to some pittance of a price, so our household was forever poor. At the end of each month, he and my mother would go to the city to sell his latest creations, so during that time, Komekko and I were latchkey children.

They'd said they would be leaving this morning, and I didn't expect to see them again for several days. I was confident there must not be much to eat in the cold room where we kept our ingredients. And that meant...

"Komekko. Let's take a little walk, okay? We'll try to get some f—"

Chomp.

"Mrgrah!"

...There was a sort of biting sound, and Ink gave a little yelp.

"...Did you just bite Ink?"

"She doesn't taste good raw."

I would have a crisis on my hands soon.

"Now listen, Komekko. Your targets are the older men. I'll use my overwhelming attractiveness to work on the young ones."

"Sis, you sly demon!"

"Heh-heh-heh, just you watch, Komekko. I didn't want to have to do this, but the state of our cold room compels me... Oh, and here comes our first mark."

Komekko held Ink like a stuffed toy as I led her by the hand toward our chosen target, acting the part of the responsible older sister.

"Well, if it isn't Bukkororii, you dashing son of a cobbler. Good morning! Lovely out, isn't it?"

"...Just FYI, I don't have a job and I don't have any money."

Thus Bukkororii, who had been practicing his dramatic poses in the courtyard, tried to take the initiative, regarding my broad smile with suspicion. I had assumed he was just another NEET; I would have to be careful not to take him too lightly in the future.

"Perish the thought. Would I ever try to scam you, Bukkororii, whom I respect so highly and to whom I've been indebted since my youngest days, out of your cash? I'm just a little hungry, that's all."

"Respect, my foot. You might as well be carrying a sign that says *moocher*. I'm unemployed and barely making ends meet myself; I'm not about to be like, 'Oh yeah, let me run home and get you some food!' Sorry, but you just have to try someone e—"

"Big Bro, I'm soooo hungry!"

"Just wait right there, Komekko! Bro'll go get you something right away!"

As I watched Bukkororii run back to his house, I turned to my little sister. "...I believe from this day forth, you may adopt the name of Komekko, the sly demon."

"My name is Komekko! She who is entrusted with watching the house and slyest demon of the little sisters of the Crimson Magic Clan!"

My demonic little sister went on to wheedle us a lot more gifts that day.

6

"Megumin! You understand, don't you?!"

No sooner had I entered the classroom than I was accosted by Yunyun, who was once again far more excited than was warranted this early in the morning.

"What I understand is that it's time for breakfast. I'll need enough for my friend here, as well."

"What do you mean, 'time for breakfast'?! Why do you assume I'll lose every single d…? Huh? When you say your 'friend,' do you mean Ink? I'm supposed to make breakfast for her now, too?!"

While Yunyun jabbered in early-morning delirium, I lifted Ink off her perch on my shoulder and held her up for all to see. "If you refuse, I will understand. However, my household is not blessed with many resources, so if you say no, this sweet thing is sure to waste away until she starves to—"

"Okay! All right, I get it; I just have to make breakfast for Ink, right?! B-but she only gets to eat if you beat me, Megumin! And if you're going to demand more food, then you have to let me set the terms of our contest today!"

"Fine by me."

"And if you won't let me, then…… What? You agree?" Yunyun looked astonished.

"Yes, it's okay," I said. "You're more than welcome to decide the nature of our competition."

"…!" Yunyun's face lit up and she pumped her fist. In the middle of it, though, she suddenly frowned. "This is our one and only contest, okay? You won't say later that I only got to set the terms of the first of a best of three, will you?!"

"I would never. What do you take me for?" I said immediately, but Yunyun still looked suspicious.

"'What you just defeated isn't my true form. The body I wear now is merely temporary. When you have defeated my next form, then and only then can you be said to be victorious, Yunyun'…is not something you're going to say anymore, right?"

"You still remember that? That was ages ago. And incidentally, I have fully four separate forms, but today, if you defeat me even once, I shall acknowledge my loss."

At that, Yunyun finally seemed to relax a little. "Right… All right!

The contest is arm wrestling! There's no way I can lose against your puny little limbs, Megumin!"

Yunyun braced her arm on her desk and rolled up her sleeve, smiling confidently. I set Ink on a corner of the desk where Yunyun would be sure to see her, then rolled up my own sleeve and sat down.

When we clasped hands, it attracted the attention of our long-legged, eye-patched classmate Arue, who came over to have a look.

"Arue, perfect timing," I said. "May we ask you to referee for us?"

Arue raised her eye patch dramatically and sat on the floor in a formal sitting position. "…Hmm, very well. Before my magic eye, no misdeed shall go unnoticed. On your marks, then…!"

"Incidentally, Yunyun. I know you're going to feed Ink-kichi and me when I win this time, but I'm afraid I still don't have a skill-up potion today. What do you want for winning?"

"Huh?! What do I want?! W-well, uh, that's a good question… Okay, how about… S-starting tomorrow morning, you and I will walk to school togeth—"

Arue, resting her hands and chin on the desk as she sat on the ground, exclaimed, "Fight!"

"Hiyah!"

"What? Ahhhh! Wait! Ohhh!"

I tried to finish the contest in one fell swoop at Arue's ambush of a start call, but Yunyun managed to just hold me off. She was physically stronger than I was, and she started to push her way back up.

If surprise had failed, then that left…!

"Hrgh… It looks like I might…have to go without breakfast this morning… Your delicious meals have always brought a small spark of joy to my day, Yunyun, but I guess…"

"?! Th-that won't work on me, okay?! Today is the day I beat you, Megumin! And then the title of Greatest Genius of the Crimson Magic Clan will be mine! I won't just be 'Yunyun, the chief's daughter' anymore…!"

Yunyun didn't like being given special treatment just because she was the daughter of the chief. I think part of the reason she harassed me every day had to do with the fact that there was no one else brave enough to go toe to toe with her.

But the name of Greatest Genius of the Crimson Magic Clan—that I would never surrender…!

"Hrgh… At this rate, it seems not only I but Ink-suke, too, shall go without food…! Our household is so poor, we can't feed another mouth, even one as small as Ink-taro's. For the sake of our dear Ink-bei, I must…not…lose…!"

"What?! Y-you… But how can she be so important to you if you can't seem to remember her name for two sentences?! You're trying to get to me! You just want to take advantage of me, right?!"

Yes, and it seemed to be working. I could feel Yunyun getting weaker. The stalemate didn't escape Arue's watchful eye.

"They're in a stalemate! Thirty seconds left! If a winner isn't decided in that time, both of you die!"

""What?!""

Neither of us had expected that particular house rule. Ink got up and walked across the desk to Yunyun. She started sweetly sniffing the arm Yunyun was using to fight me.

"S-stop that, Ink… Don't worry—I'll feed you even if I win…! Just don't act so cute…!"

"What belongs to a pet belongs to her owner! Know that if I have no food, I shall steal Ink's!"

"You monster!"

"The winner: Megumin!" Arue announced, holding my right arm aloft.

7

"I believe you have heard that one of the village NEETs…er, a brave young person with time on their hands…was able to drive the monsters away from the village. Thanks to their hard work, there are currently no powerful monsters in the vicinity. We specifically asked them to leave the weaker monsters and only exterminate the most dangerous ones. On that note, we're taking a field trip today to get some battle experience. We're going to raise everyone's level in a relatively safe environment via a time-tested Crimson Magic Clan technique called farming. Everyone, assemble in the courtyard! Form three groups of three and one pair! Get going!"

Such was the plan our teacher outlined after calling attendance. It provoked a lot of chatter in the classroom as soon as he exited the classroom. While everyone else was finding their best friends to team up with, Yunyun sat at her desk, stealing occasional glances in my direction.

"What is it? O self-proclaimed rival of mine, Yunyun."

"Self-proclaimed?! Er... I mean... I am, I guess... He says to make groups."

"So he does. Groups, eh? What about it?"

I deliberately kept my response cool and watched as Yunyun started to trip over herself.

...*My goodness.*

It looked like she still couldn't bring herself even to say that she wanted to work with me. Well, I did take her breakfast. Maybe I could give her this one.

"Hey, Megumin, if you don't have anyone to work with, how about me?"

My invitation to Yunyun was preempted by Arue, who had shown up out of nowhere.

But the teacher had said we should be in groups of three, right?

"Very well," I said. "Let us work together."

"?!" Beside me, Yunyun looked even more distressed. Arue and I gave her a casual glance.

At last Yunyun said hesitantly, "U-um, Megumin, could I...?"

But she never got to finish.

*   *   *

"Heeey, Yunyun, you're gonna work with us, right?"

"Yeah, you never have a partner, right? We'll let you join us."

Funifura and Dodonko called out to Yunyun. They came over to her seat, both grinning.

"Oh, er… But…" Yunyun, not sure what to do, shot a glance at Arue and me.

"Come on, Yunyun—let's go. We're classmates!"

"Yeah, we're friends, aren't we?"

"?! F-f-friends…! W-well, okay then…" Yunyun stood up, her face bright red on account of that one word.

Easy! An easier target I'd never seen.

I had a very bad feeling about the kind of men she would fall for in the future.

Yunyun still had half an eye on us as she let Funifura usher her out of the classroom.

As we watched her go, Arue whispered…

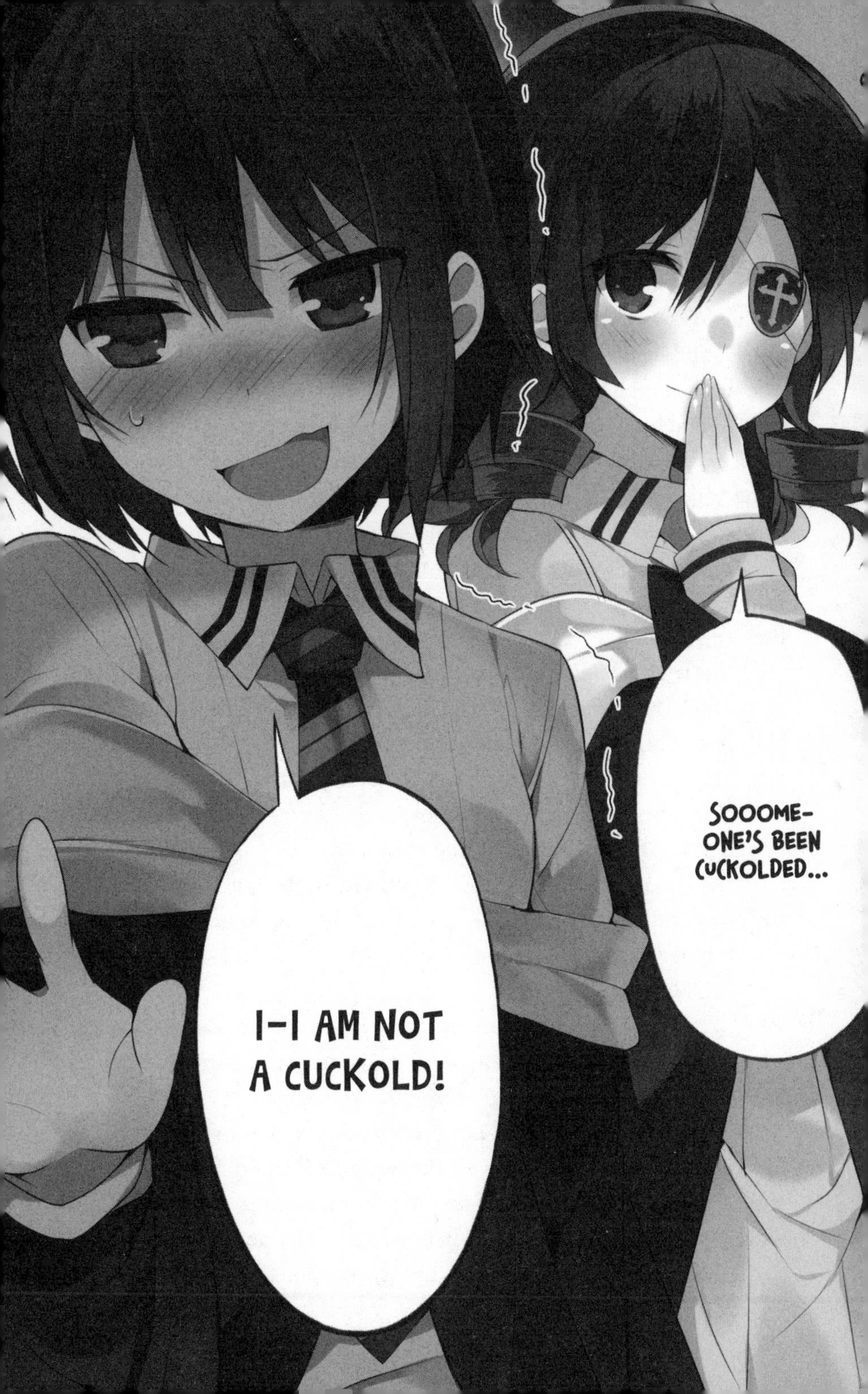
SOOOME-ONE'S BEEN CUCKOLDED...
I-I AM NOT A CUCKOLD!

8

Outside, our teacher gave a flourish of his cape and said, "Good, I see everyone's here! Those who have weapons already, feel free to use them. If you don't have a weapon, use this to finish off those monsters!"

He indicated something on the ground: a mountain of armaments. The main thing I noticed, though, was...

"T-Teacher! All these weapons look too big to hold..."

Yes, the weapons were gigantic. There were great swords longer than Arue was tall, axes with blades wider than my shoulders. A morning star with a ball so big, an ogre couldn't have swung it...

As we looked on, our scrawny teacher hefted a massive great sword as if it were light as a feather. He used only one hand. He didn't even break a sweat...!

"The trick is to direct the magical energy that resides in your body into all the fibers of your muscles. By doing so, we Crimson Magic Clan folk are able to temporarily grant ourselves a boost in strength. Believe it or not, my class has been about pounding into you the basics that will allow you to do this. Now, just focus, and you'll be able to access that power naturally!"

Arue took a step forward. And then...

"**...O magical energy that flows through me, grant strength unto my limbs!**" she shouted...and then with one hand, she picked up a sword that was bigger than she was!

""""Ooh!""""

"What?! Th-that's incredible...! But was that speech really necessary?!"

The other students, pretending they hadn't heard Yunyun's less than reverent remark, swarmed the weapons.

"**This precious one will not buckle, even if I pour into her every ounce of the magical energy in my body...! Behold, for now I name thee! From this day forth, thou shalt be known as...!**" One student with a gigantic halberd in hand bellowed out a name.

Another girl was swinging a single-bladed long sword with a vicious grin. **"Heh!! ...Goodness, I'm surprised you survived that practice swing. Very well, that proves I can trust you with my life...!"**

I ignored all of them and grabbed a huge ax. Considering *my* level of magical power, this should be nothing...!

"...Hrgh, it looks like I haven't summoned enough magic yet...! Flare up, magical power of mine...! Now, grant me the blessings of your strength...!"

I managed to lift the ax, stumbling backward.

Still not enough. Not enough magic!

I was the greatest genius of the Crimson Magic Clan! This should be child's play for me...!

I gritted my teeth and hefted the weapon again.

From nearby, Yunyun said, "T-Teacher, isn't this all just an act...? These weapons are made from wood with metal plating, and they're all *really* light..."

"That's five points off your score, Yunyun."

"What?! B-but, Teacher!"

I flung the ax aside and grabbed the smallest wooden sword I could find.

We were in the woods outside the village, lined up in front of the teacher, each of us holding our preferred armament. Most of what we were carrying amounted to various blunt instruments. Only Yunyun had a proper weapon: the silver dagger she'd bought from the smith the other day.

"All right! Listen up, you runts. Like I said, the bigger monsters have been run out of town. All that's left is nice, easy prey. And just to be extra sure about this, I've gone through and put magical binding spells on everything in the area. Your job is to go out there and finish off those immobilized monsters." The teacher was still carrying his gigantic—but fake—sword. "I don't expect any problems, but if anything does come up, just shout extra loudly. Okay, get going!"

The teacher went jogging off to who knows where, and my classmates scattered.

Then we heard a voice from the direction our teacher had gone: "*Freeze Bind*!"

Arue and I turned toward the sound and…

""Ooh…""

…were reminded that as half-baked as he might be, our teacher was still a member of the Crimson Magic Clan.

Specifically, we saw an oversize lizard, crying piteously and frozen from the neck down.

"*Freeze Bind*!"

There was our teacher's voice again in the distance. He was happily immobilizing all the nearby monsters.

Arue and I looked at each other.

"Can I go first?" Arue whispered, and I nodded.

She took the huge—but fake—sword and held it above her head with both hands. "Offer up thy lifeblood to feed my power!"

The sword came down on the lizard's head; the frozen creature squeaked once and went limp.

Arue checked her Adventurer's Card and nodded in satisfaction: It looked like she had gained a level.

I needed four more skill points in order to learn Explosion. If I finished off everything here, I might just be able to learn the spell before I left school today!

I scanned the area for any possible source of experience points and spotted a group standing in front of a big horned rabbit. They seemed to be discussing something rather animatedly.

Then I saw her: Yunyun, standing there in front of the rabbit, her silver dagger ready but motionless. She was, it seemed, unable to strike the finishing blow against the rabbit, which looked at her sadly and whimpered "*Kyuu, kyuu*" as if begging for its life. Yunyun's groupmates were trying their best to encourage her.

"Y-Yunyun, hurry up and do it in! We have to move on to the next one!"

"Sh-she's right. You've got the second-best grades in class, Yunyun; you have to show us how it's done!"

Yunyun shook her head tearfully. "I'm… I'm sorry! Our eyes met…! I'm sorry—I can't do it!" She returned the dagger in its sheath and held it out to the girls, but neither of them took it.

"It's a little late for that! Us Crimson Magic Clan folk, we can't be, like, soft, you know? People would make fun of us!"

"Y-y-yeah, yeah. It's easy—that thing's not even moving. Show us the power of the second-best student in class! Just be like, *zap!* and…!"

"*Zap!* it is, then."

I came up behind Dodonko, one of Yunyun's groupmates, pushing her forward.

"Huh?! Watch it!" she exclaimed.

I took the dagger from Yunyun and pressed it into the flustered Dodonko's hand. Almost hugging her from behind, I wrapped her fingers firmly around the hilt, then made her hold it in front of her. And then…

"Now, Dodonko! Finish it! Tear this pitiful, misty-eyed bunny apart and gain the experience it offers!"

"Wait! Hey, hold on! Megumin, stop, I'm sorry!"

"What are you hesitating for? Sacrifice this innocent rabbit's life…! Your guide now is not Yunyun, the second-best student in class, but myself, the very leader in grades…!"

"Nooo! Stop, please stop! If you keep pushing, I'll really cut it! Can't you hear it crying? Can't you hear it going 'Kyuu, kyuu'?!"

Funifura waded in to try to stop me. "Hey, Megumin, stoppit! You're making Dodonko cry! St— I said stop it already!"

"…Girls? I think there's something a lot nastier than a rabbit out there."

Arue was pointing toward the woods.

We looked where she was pointing, and there was a monster. It was a humanoid demon with sharp claws on both hands, pitch-black fur, and wings like a bat. There was a birdlike beak on its reptilian face, and it was looking this way and that with close attention to everything around it.

There were a number of issues, such as the fact that it looked awfully powerful, but the single biggest problem was that it wasn't encased in ice.

This was the moment to quietly back away and go get the teacher...

At least, that was the plan until the monster looked right at us.

9

""Teacherteacherteacherteacher——!!""

Funifura and Dodonko shouted at the top of their lungs as they went running.

"Megumin, do you know that thing? It seems awfully interested in you," Arue said.

"How could I possibly *know* a thing like that? It must be a foot soldier of the Demon King, terrified of the power hidden within me... S-seriously, though, why is it chasing me?!"

"What goes around comes around! I saw you nibbling on the offering left on the altar in the Eris Church the other day, you know!" Yunyun informed me.

They were running to the other side of me as we fled the monster. The creature, flying through the air, showed no interest at all in anyone else. For some reason, it was coming straight after me. I was sure it could see the other students. I was starting to worry that Yunyun was right and this was some sort of punishment.

Arue and I had long ago abandoned our oversize weapons, which were only going to make it harder to run. Members of the other groups spotted what was going on, but considering that no one in any of them could use magic...!

Then I felt something squirming at my back. It was Ink, digging in her claws and holding on for dear life.

That's it!

I peeled the cat off my back and held her up high so the monster could see her.

"I can see I have no choice. I offer you this fur ball! How about it? Looks tastier than me, right? So tasty, even my little sister wants to eat her!"

"That's our top student! You sure have some unique ideas!"

"You're awful! You want to know why a monster is chasing you? It's because you're always doing things like this!"

I ignored Yunyun's reproof, continuing to hold Ink aloft; the monster circled in midair and then settled to the ground in front of us. As terrible as the creature looked, it didn't act especially hostile. With the other students looking on—except Funifura and Dodonko, who were long gone—I confronted the creature.

Then, suddenly, Yunyun was standing in front of me. She gripped her dagger in both hands, the silver blade glinting, facing down the beast to protect Arue and me.

Yunyun was the only one around with a real weapon. And it looked like she intended to protect us from this demon even though she hadn't had the heart to kill so much as a small, helpless bunny.

Beside me, Arue glanced at her own Adventurer's Card. She was trying to see if there were any powerful spells she could learn right here and now.

…Me, I could already have acquired Advanced Magic. But if I did that, then Explosion would be…

But could I let timid, introverted Yunyun look better than me…?!

"O dark bolt, pierce mine enemy! *Cursed Lightning!*"

The shout produced a bolt of black lightning that slammed into the monster's chest. The creature collapsed without so much as a cry. But we ignored it and looked in the direction of the voice to see our teacher walking toward us at a leisurely pace, the giant sword resting on his shoulder.

Our teacher had a tendency to cause more problems than he solved, but he really came through for us this time and even looked cool doing it.

Beside him were our classmates, who must have gone to get him.

"Teacher, you already finished the incantation. So why did you wait till the last minute to cast the spell?!"

"? Because you always wait until the coolest moment to rescue someone, obviously."

...Okay, so he caused a *lot* more problems than he solved.

10

"Hey, did you hear? The monster that attacked Megumin—they say there's never been one like it around here before. There aren't supposed to be any flying monsters near the village."

After my little adventure with the monster, our field trip had been hastily cut short, and we had been ushered back to the school. But almost as soon as we were back, the rumors started flying.

I was eavesdropping on the conversation, absentmindedly tugging on Ink's tail where she sat on my desk, when the teacher came in looking unusually tired. His shoulders slumped as he stood at the lectern.

"Listen up, all of you. You remember I told you about the trouble with the seal on the Dark God's tomb? And I think most of you saw the creature we encountered outside this morning. Our investigation suggests it might have been a servant of the Dark God. It was looking for the pieces of the seal but didn't find any. In light of this, we have to continue investigating, and fast. They're going to need my help. It's another monster hunt for me, just like yesterday... As such, classes will be canceled again this afternoon. Like I told you before, until the tomb is completely resealed, don't go home alone. Travel in groups. Class dismissed!"

Then the teacher left the room.

I didn't know anything about any Dark God. I only knew that this was a pain in the neck.

Yunyun glanced at me and said hesitantly, "Megumin… U-um, m-maybe you'd like to…"

Sheesh, all she had to do was ask to go home together.

"Yunyun," I said, "would you like to go—?"

"Hey, Yunyun," Funifura interrupted, "let's go home together! Actually, there's something I want to talk to you about! And I want to apologize for ditching you earlier!"

"What?! Uh… S-sure." Yunyun, who had never been one to resist peer pressure, immediately nodded. I renewed my concern at how eager she was to go with the flow. I kept imagining some strange man begging and pleading and Yunyun doing anything he asked.

"Um, w-well, I guess that's that, Megumin. See you tomorrow…"

Yunyun trailed after Funifura and Dodonko out of the classroom, looking strangely anxious and lonely.

………

It was a *good* thing that Yunyun, seemingly destined to be alone, had made some friends.

Yes, it was good, and yet, somehow…

I felt something behind me and turned. It was Arue, looking like she could hardly restrain herself.

"……………**Cuck—**"

"If you utter one more syllable, those huge, detestable boobs of yours shall meet a terrible fate!"

11

The next day.

I came into the classroom with Ink, who was riding on my shoulder. For a cat, she seemed awfully friendly.

"Oh, morning, Megumin… And morning, Ink."

Yunyun, who usually confronted me with a challenge the moment she saw me, greeted me normally this second for some reason.

"Yes, good morning," I said. "What's wrong? Normally you leap on me like a highway bandit spoiling for a fight the second you see my face."

"Have I been that rough?! Er, I mean, you're not exactly wrong, but what a way to put it… Like a friendly competition between rivals…"

Two girls appeared beside the sputtering Yunyun: Funifura and Dodonko.

"Mornin', Yunyun! Thanks for yesterday, huh? That was a big help! Friends really are the best, huh?"

"Yeah, thanks! We knew we could count on you, Yunyun!"

"U-um, I'm sure glad I could help out my friends…!" Yunyun's face shone with a smile.

…I wonder what happened here.

"All right, get to your seats, everybody! I'm going to take attendance!"

The teacher arrived before I had decided whether to ask Yunyun what was going on.

After roll call, the teacher wrote a magical incantation on the blackboard.

It took more than skill points to learn magic. First, you had to learn the entire chant or incantation for the spell you wanted. And unlike basic magic, which hardly had incantations, learning the words to invoke advanced magic took some real time.

As for me, the head of the class, though, I had already learned all the relevant chants. And so had the class's second-best student, Yunyun, who was sitting beside me, as bored as I was. I decided to pester her a little.

Did something happen with Funifura and Dodonko yesterday? I wrote on the edge of some notebook paper. Then I balled it up and flicked it over to Yunyun's desk.

Yunyun read the note, then wrote one of her own and sent it flying back:

Sorry, friends can't reveal their secrets to their rivals.

.........Now, that ticked me off.

For a girl who never had a friend her entire life, a couple of days with some new besties have sure made you feel self-important, I wrote.

Look who's talking, Megumin—you aren't exactly swimming in friends yourself, she sent back.

I glanced in her direction and found her smirking triumphantly at me.

....

So you made some new friends... Now I see why you stopped challenging me. As happy as I am that you finally have someone to care about, the flip side is I've become a bit lonely...

Wait—I'm sorry. I'm sorry, okay? That's not what I meant by not challenging you! It's just that a lot happened yesterday, and I wasn't really feeling like it...!

Please, please, you mustn't worry about me. But whatever I may have said, I actually quite look forward to our morning battles, you know. And not just as a source of free lunch.

I'm sorry! Really! That's really, really not what I meant! I enjoyed our battles, too, and I even enjoyed making your lunch every day...!

...It is enough for me just to hear that from you. If only we weren't rivals, I truly think we might have been excellent friends.

....

After I sent that note, Yunyun stopped answering.

When I glanced over, her face was bright red, and she wasn't writing anything. If I squinted, though, I could just make out what was on her paper.

Megumin, someday I hope we can be...fr

She seemed to have stopped right in the middle of writing.

Inspired by the sight of her, I jotted one more note and sent it flying over, making sure it landed where she would notice it.

The red-faced girl snapped her head up suddenly when she saw it. Her eyes were swimming with expectation and maybe hope as she opened the note...!

...Wow, I really had you going there, huh? Dummy!

Yunyun kicked back her chair, jumped up, and attacked me, weeping all the while.

12

Yunyun and I were still arguing in the courtyard in front of the school.

"...Goodness. I have never met someone so oblivious to a joke."

"Joke, indeed! I'll never forgive you! Never!"

Thanks to Yunyun's tearful lunge at me, we had been kicked out of our previous class and had spent the entire period standing out in the hallway as punishment. Now it was gym class, and we were allegedly practicing for battle.

"You there! Quit jabbering, unless you want to spend this hour standing around, too. I don't care how many incantations you've memorized—I don't want you interfering with the other students' learning. Twenty points off for each of you! ...Okay. It's time to practice your fighting skills, girls. But our training today is going to have a twist... You two, the ones having a staring contest over there! I have a question for you. What's the most important thing for surviving combat?"

Yunyun took a step forward. I could tell, though, that she was still intensely aware of me.

"Friends, sir!" she said. "If you have friends, your chances of survival increase dramatically! Not including so-called 'friends' who are so dumb that they don't understand there are some things you don't do even as a joke!"

...C-curse that girl...!

"Hmm... Next, Megumin! What do you think is the most important thing for surviving combat?"

"Firepower, sir! Enough firepower to blow away the enemy and any lonely milquetoasts who parade around blathering about friends! Strength! Overwhelming force! I seek to become a proud, independent wizard, rather than to go around scrounging for 'friends' and 'companions'!"

"Grrrr…!" Yunyun was once again looking at me through tears.

The teacher crossed his arms and nodded, considering our answers.

""How many points, sir?!"" we chorused.

"Three points each," he said. "I'm disappointed! I'm disappointed in both of you! Sit down and listen up! …**Pfeh!**" And then the teacher *spat!*

Ugh! I was even angrier with this teacher than I was with Yunyun!

We seated ourselves formally on the ground as instructed. The teacher ignored our furious shaking and bellowed, "Arue! I'm sure *you* know the answer! Unlike certain *so-called* Crimson Magic Clan folk who have nothing but grades to boast of!"

So-called Crimson Magic Clan folk!

Yunyun and I both ground our teeth.

At length, Arue took a step forward. Then she flipped up the patch covering her eye and—

"**It's the prebattle speech, sir.** If you get that right, then you could be fighting a million-man army with only a radish for a weapon and emerge victorious. Otherwise, even if you were the almighty Demon King, you will be more likely to die if you exclaim, 'Let me give you one final gift on your way to hell!' or 'Your chances of beating me are a measly 0.1 percent!'"

"Full score! You've got a skill-up potion coming your way later! I assume you've memorized the Clan's *Famous Quotes for Not Dying*? All right, everybody, pair up and practice your speeches!"

Everyone started pairing up with their favorite classmates.

There was just one problem: This class had eleven people in it.

I had cut gym before, so we'd had an even number, but I didn't feel like trying to play hooky today. I hauled myself up off the ground and turned to Yunyun, who was still sitting beside me. "...Yunyun, let's work together. I assume Funifura and Dodonko will pair up anyway. Come on—that would make you the odd one out, wouldn't it?"

"...Fine, Megumin, let's work together. Just don't think this is going to stop at some speeches!"

It looked like we both had the same idea.

"Teacher, we're going to have one extra. Could you work with me?"

"Fine with me, Arue... Okay, everyone, get started!"

So while our classmates had friendly face-offs, Yunyun and I alone confronted each other with utmost seriousness.

"It looks like the time has come to settle this," I said. "I place my faith in this: that she who has put in the hard work shall at last emerge victorious. I come from nothing, but I have taken my journey one step at a time... Against you, the chief's daughter, born and raised in luxury, I cannot lose! I shall prove that it is not background or even talent but sheer tenacity that wins the day!"

"And me, I've never defeated you even one single, solitary time... But even if my chances of beating you may be virtually nothing...as long as they aren't *absolutely* nothing, then I will never give up!"

Thus, we both announced our unshakable resolve. And then...

"".........""

Then we just stood there silently, looking at each other.

"...What was that? That's unfair, stealing the hero's lines like that! Now I practically feel as if *I* will lose! What happened to all your talk of friendship? Say something more along those lines!"

"What about you, Megumin? After that whole speech about fire-power, you can't say something more villainous? What was all that about hard work anyway? You're practically the picture of the gifted genius! And that was a low blow, bringing my family into it!"

The prebattle speech allegedly improved one's chances of victory. But this time-tested secret technique of the Crimson Magic Clan didn't mean anything when your opponent was another Crimson Magic Clan member…!

"I have had enough of this! Is this combat training or not? Let us settle this with our fists! Then there will be nothing more to say!"

"Sounds good to me! But do you really think you can win, Megumin, being so much smaller than I am? I'm warning you—your little tricks won't work today!"

And then Yunyun tried to get the upper hand by striking first! She launched a gentle kick at my midriff to keep me at bay. It also allowed her to judge the distance between us; then she planted her feet and kicked off the ground…!

"Mrrrow!"

The voice from my midriff froze Yunyun in mid-leap.

Okay, so it wasn't technically from my midriff but more like from my clothes.

Ink had burrowed into my robes and was mewling at having been kicked by Yunyun, however gently.

"Oh… Ohhh…" The moment Yunyun realized what had happened, she was in a complete tizzy.

"What's wrong? You look so confused. If you're done attacking, then I shall take my turn!"

I slid closer, but Yunyun backed away anxiously. "No, wait! Please wait! Don't hold Ink! Then I can't attack you!"

"What will you do now, Yunyun, with all your talk of friendship? Friends don't always just help you in the heat of battle, you know. Sometimes they serve very well as hostages or to get you in trouble! As for me, I'll happily blow away friend and foe alike with my firepower! Come on—attack me if you can! If you can kick this cat, whom you named, then kick away!"

"You're the wooooorst!"

13

On the way home, after I had defeated Yunyun in our little contest.

"Megumin, you've never once fought fair in one of our competitions!"

"And here I thought we agreed to let things go after that battle. You certainly are one to hold a grudge, Yunyun!" Personally, I was trying to go home by myself, but Yunyun, on the pretext that it was dangerous until the Dark God was sealed back in its tomb, insisted on following me, arguing the entire time. "Anyway, it's your refusal to tell me what went on with the girls that has me bent out of shape. Was it that embarrassing? Surely you could at least give me a hint?"

"It—it wasn't embarrassing! And no, I couldn't. I refuse to reveal someone else's secrets! Friends have to be able to trust each other!"

How naive this girl was. I could safely declare: In the future, Yunyun would definitely fall in with some worthless man.

I would have to make sure that didn't happen.

"...Very well, then. But, Yunyun—and I mean no disrespect to your friends when I say this—I haven't heard very good things about them, you know? I don't know what's going on, but I think a little skepticism would do you some good."

"You're too suspicious, Megumin. Whatever happened to you to make you doubt people?"

"Doubt is the first thing you must do in a family situation like mine. Living on a razor's edge as we do, if you get taken in by some scheme, the entire household could find itself on the street before you know what's happening. Why, just the other day, my sister tells me, some shop owner came by claiming that my father's worthless magical inventions were all brilliant. Can you believe it?"

"W-well... I have to admit, even I think that's probably a scam..."

This amounted to a tacit admission that Yunyun agreed that my father's ideas were junk, but that was a sting I would just have to take.

Consider, for example, a magic scroll, which, when read aloud in a dark place, would light up the surrounding area. It sounds very convenient. But how can you read the scroll if it's already dark? And it turns out that if there's even the slightest light around, the scroll won't work. It makes no sense.

That wasn't all. There was the potion that exploded when you opened it, the potion that exploded when it was subject to any kind of impact, and other completely unfathomable creations.

It's wonderful to make a living from your passion, but it would be even better to *make a living* at all.

...Then again, as someone eager to learn Explosion, which was widely regarded as a parlor trick, maybe I wasn't one to judge.

Finally, we got within sight of my house...

"...Let me tell you, I think perhaps you needn't worry so much about having absolutely no friends at all. You might be surprised. Maybe there's someone around you right now who understands you better than you think."

Such was the advice I delivered to the befuddled Yunyun before going home...

...or trying to, whereupon I noticed a suspicious-looking man loitering in front of my house.

"H-hey, Megumin, who's that?!"

"He's trying to look in the windows, it seems. It must be some stalker who... Hmm?"

I knew that man peering into the windows of my house. It was Bukkororii, the cobbler's son who had too much time on his hands. If he had some business with me, he should have just boldly announced himself.

"What is it you're doing there?"

"Yipes?! Oh, uh, Megumin... Great, I've been waiting for you. There's something I wanted to ask you about. But look, it's already late today... Tomorrow's a holiday, so there's no school, right? So how about tomorrow morning...? Well, if possible, I'd like to have Yunyun come,

too. I absolutely need the perspective of some young women on this."
He scratched his head in embarrassment.

Yunyun and I looked at each other...

"I'm hooome!"

"Welcome home, Sis!" Komekko came sprinting into the room, feet pounding.

"Are you hungry?" I asked with a smile. "I shall make something for you right now."

Komekko, though, shook her head. "I'm not hungry. I had lots to eat."

...Lots to eat?

We didn't have lots to eat anywhere in our house. I would have found this pronouncement thoroughly unsettling had I left Ink at home that day, but she was riding safely on my shoulder. Perplexed, I headed for the kitchen...

There, I was struck dumb by a huge pile of food.

Vegetables, fruits, sweets. There were even some toys mixed in.

"Tell me: Where did you get all this?"

At that, Komekko gave me a very serious look.

"My name is Komekko! She who is entrusted with watching the house and slyest demon of the little sisters of the Crimson Magic Clan!"

Then she struck a pose.

This girl has a bright, bright future ahead of her.

Lady Komekko and the Great Lord Host

"Hey, you're a little late today. Let's get cracking." Host was sitting in front of the tomb of the Dark God again. "I was so sure there was just one seal puzzle, but I guess I was wrong... Hey, Komekko. Today we're gonna break Lady Wolbach's seal for real. It's your time to shine, girl."

"Okay," I replied. When we had solved the first puzzle, a more difficult one showed up from inside the pedestal.

"Check this out: I brought you more food. I mean, it's just something I caught outside the village and then grilled up. I can't exactly go shoppin' in town. Hope you can live with this." Then he presented me with some sort of very cooked meat...

"...*Drool.*"

"...For when you've made some progress on that puzzle, all right? But look, why're you even here? Ain'tcha got a mommy or some friends or something?"

"Mom's never home, and I'm the only girl my age in the village. I don't have any toys, either, so I was playing with this."

"...I get it. Well, uh. Anyway, the Great Lord Host is here if you want to talk, at least till you finish that puzzle. This one looks pretty tough, so I bet it'll take you a while. Security's pretty tight around the village, so I can't get here every day, but I'll bring you something to eat when I can." He took a look at my work. "Hey, you're comin' along."

"Uh-huh." I had swallowed my drool and gotten to work.

"…You thinkin' about this?"

"…Uh-huh."

He had noticed me glancing at the meat while I worked. Now he grinned. "For a demon, a contract is absolute. I said this was for when you'd made some progress on the puzzle, right?"

I stopped and glanced at him. "You're so cool, Host."

"Flattery won't get you anywhere, sweet cheeks."

"…I haven't had solid food in three days."

"I saw you scarf down the stuff I brought you yesterday. The woe-is-me act won't work on me."

"I'm going to be an even more awesome wizard than my big sis. You'd best not make me any angrier…"

"You got a big mouth for such a little kid. You know threats don't work on a demon, right?" Now he was really grinning.

"…I'm too hungry to think anymore, so fork over the food. Please, Great Lord Host?"

"Heh! Geez, guess I ain't got any choice! Here, eat up, Komekko!"

He hadn't done anything to prepare the food he'd hunted but put some salt on it, but it was still delicious.

When I had finished the hunk of meat, Host said, "Okay. Now we know who rules the roost, and your tummy should be nice and full. So listen to your Great Lord Host, Komekko, and solve that puzzle."

"…I'm too full. I'm sleepy now."

"Grrr! Don't you piss me off! You can't do that to me after you scarfed down my food! Listen to me, Komekko!"

I just flopped down on my stomach on the ground, fiddling with the puzzle even as I drifted off to sleep. "Yeah, I'm full, but I still don't wanna work on it."

"…P-please, please tackle that puzzle for me, Lady Komekko…"

"Heh! Geez, guess I ain't got any choice!"

"H-hey, kids don't get to say that! Even if you did learn it from me!"

Chapter
3

Guardians

1

"Morning, Megumin. Have you had breakfast?"

"Good morning. Recently, my little sister has been wheedling gifts out of people. I've been having the scraps, so I'm quite full, thank you."

"And... And you're *okay* with that?"

Today was a holiday for the Crimson Magic Clan, so there was no school.

It wasn't exactly perfect weather; the sky was overcast. Yunyun and I were together first thing, on our way to find out what Bukkororii wanted.

"Heh-heh, just take a look at this, Megumin!" Yunyun gleefully showed me something.

It was a board game. A game of combat that, as I recalled, was popular in the capital.

"And what about it?"

"My uncle was on a trip to the capital, and he brought it back for me. He said, 'It's impossible to play this by yourself, so maybe it'll help even *you*...' I didn't really understand what he meant, though."

...I supposed Yunyun's uncle had a lot to worry about, in his own way.

"I'm thinking about bringing it to school, but do you want to try it while we're waiting for Bukkororii?"

"...I suppose I do not mind. Though I doubt I will lose a game of intellectual prowess, yes?"

So we set up the game on the grass.

"Okay," Yunyun said, "I'll go first...!"

Thirty minutes later.

"Grrrrr! H-here! I'll move my Sword Master into this space right here!"

"I'm teleporting my Arch-wizard to *this* space."

"I hate how you use Teleport, Megumin! ...Hey, how about we agree not to use the Arch-wizard?"

"I will agree to no such thing. Oh look, you're in check."

"Aaaargh! Wait, wait!"

And after an hour...

"F-finally! If I can keep this up, I think I can eke out a win...! All right, Megumin, your end is near! I'm moving my Crusader to this sp—"

"*Explooosion!*"

"Ahhh! Megumin, that's no fair, flipping the board over like that!"

"Of course it is. It's even in the rule book. Right here: 'When the Arch-wizard is on her home square...'"

After two hours.

"One more round! Please, Megumin, just one more!"

"No matter how many times we play, I always win. Just admit it and give up... I must say, though, this game is quite interesting. I assert my victor's right to borrow it for a while."

"Oh! W-wait! Ugh, the rules of this game are so weird! Explosion? Teleport? Who came up with this thing?" Yunyun, her eyes brimming, sent one of the pieces flying with a flick of her finger.

"I cannot help noticing that the man who called this meeting is himself late. What could Bukkororii be up to?"

"...Should we go call him?"

Thus, we ended up at Bukkororii's house, which wasn't far away.

His place was the number one cobbler in the village. Then again, it was the only shoe repair shop in the village.

When we entered, we were greeted by the proprietor, namely, Bukkororii's dad.

"Pardon us," I said. "Would Bukkororii happen to be here?"

"Oh, Megumin, it's you. Welcome! If you're looking for my boy, he's still asleep."

...Ahem.

"Well, if you'll excuse my asking, could you wake him for us? As a matter of fact, he told us, *'There's something I'd like to ask a couple of sweet young girls like you... Pant, pant...!'*"

"That son of mine!" Bukkororii's father immediately went storming upstairs.

"Th-that's not nice!" Yunyun exclaimed. "True, that's more or less what Bukkororii said to us but also completely different!"

"This is the least one ought to do to a NEET who calls people to a meeting and then casually oversleeps."

We heard some shrieks and bellows from upstairs, and then Bukkororii came tumbling to the main floor. "Yeeeek! Ugh, Megumin! You're the worst! My old man smacked me awake, shouting about me being a jailbait-loving bastard or something!"

"I believe it is the just deserts of those who ask for help and then sleep straight through the scheduled meeting time. Come now—let us go!"

"Hey, wait just a second! I haven't even gotten dressed!"

When we left the shop after Bukkororii had finally gotten dressed, we went to the only café in town with an unusual menu.

"Yunyun, order whatever you like. Bukkororii will be paying, so don't hesitate to get anything at all. Oh, as for me, I'll have whichever parfait has the most calories."

"Aren't you supposed to wait for me to *offer* to pay?! I hardly have any money…"

"I'm pretty full, so, uh, just water for me… Megumin, didn't you say you already ate a lot this morning?"

When we had finished ordering, we turned once more to Bukkororii to find out what he wanted.

"Sorry for dragging you out here," he said. "You might be able to guess why I'm asking for your help. The truth is, I… I'm in love!"

"What?!"

"Even though you are a shiftless NEET?!"

"Being a NEET has nothing to do with it! Even NEETs eat and sleep—and we love, too!"

Yunyun and I, however, were no longer listening.

"H-he's here about love! Megumin, he wants our advice on love!"

"I never imagined anyone in our village would accept someone so bittersweet as this… Which reminds me, who is it? Could it be someone we know, perhaps? For that matter…could it be one of us…?!"

"Hey, watch it. Think of the age difference, you two. I'm not some jailbai— H-hey, stoppit! Stop, both of you! I'm sorry, so stop trying to pour Tabasco in my coffee!"

After this flurry of apologies, though, Bukkororii suddenly turned very serious.

"…*Ahem*. So the person I'm in love with is…"

2

In light of their immense magical power, it was common for Crimson Magic Clan people to end up in magic-related jobs. They might create magical items or craft potions.

And then there was the woman with whom Bukkororii was unrequitedly in love, who ran a perfectly ordinary fortune-telling shop. Like any Crimson Magic Clanner, she loved training and spent her free time alone in the mountains practicing finishing moves.

We left the café and headed to her shop.

"I cannot believe the object of your affection is Soketto. For a NEET, you have awfully high standards."

"What, can't a NEET want the best for himself? Listen to me, Megumin—people *should* aspire to something great. Not just in love but in life, too. I want to be something more than just a cobbler…"

"But if you wish to date someone, perhaps finding some work first would be advisable…" While Bukkororii took the conversation in a strange direction, I thought about Soketto. "You are dealing with the person known as the most beautiful woman of the Crimson Magic Clan. And you are…not really known as anything. Just a NEET with no future, reluctant to take over his father's business… Look, Bukkororii, Yunyun and I will keep you company today, so how about you just give up?"

"Don't be all logical about this! Maybe she's one of those weirdos who *likes* worthless men. First we have to at least find out what her type is."

"I see you recognize that you are a worthless man. I can respect that. Eh, okay, we have time to kill. Why not give it a shot?"

"U-um, if you know you're worthless, why not make an effort to become a more worthwhile person? Not that I mind trying to find out Soketto's type…"

Bukkororii, blatantly ignoring Yunyun and me, took a few bold steps forward. It seemed he wanted us, the women, to find out from Soketto whether she was currently interested in anyone and, if not, what kind of person she *would* be interested in. That was what he had really wanted from us all along.

"I do think you could at least ask her her type by yourself. You might even stumble into an actual conversation that way."

"If I had guts—or social skills—do you think I would still be a NEET? …Ooh, there she is!"

Bukkororii sounded weirdly proud of his question but was distracted when Soketto emerged from her shop. We watched her from a distance, hidden among the trees.

In front of her fortune-telling establishment, the girl known as the most beautiful woman of the Crimson Magic Clan had a broom in hand and was sweeping away. A totally mundane activity elevated to the status of art by Soketto's sheer beauty.

"She's as gorgeous as ever… I wish I could be trash littered by her feet…"

"NEETs are already trash, so you're halfway there."

"M-Megumin!"

As we watched, Soketto took a big stretch and then, unfortunately, retreated back into her shop.

That's when it came to me: a brilliant idea.

"Bukkororii! That's it!"

"Wh-what's it? My trash strategy? Uh, I really think we should leave that freaky role-playing stuff for later in our relationship…"

"Do not be stupid; that is not what I have in mind! A superb idea just occurred to me. Soketto runs a fortune-telling shop. And they say she is very good at what she does. So have her tell your fortune! Yes: Ask her, Bukkororii, who your future lover will be!"

"Ahhh! That might just work!" Yunyun said. "If she sees herself in his future, he wouldn't have to confess his feelings, and they could start dating—simple! And if she predicts some other woman, that proves it won't work with her…"

I suppose that would all hurt a little less than confessing to her and just getting shot down.

Bukkororii, however, was not wholly on board.

"You misunderstand NEETs. If I had the money to get my fortune told, I would be in there every single day."

"I believe this means we are free to go home, yes?"

We turned to leave, causing Bukkororii to bow madly in apology.

However, there was still one problem.

"Hey, even if we go into Soketto's shop...wouldn't just asking about her type be a little...sudden?"

Very true: Bukkororii was not the only one who had never been in Soketto's shop. How were we supposed to ask such a question out of the blue?

Bukkororii crossed his arms, looking very serious. "So it's come to this. Looks like I'm gonna have to scare up the money to get my fortune told...!"

3

The vicinity of Crimson Magic Village was populated by powerful monsters, the kind the average adventurer would be hard-pressed to get away from safely, let alone fight. The pelts and internal organs of these threatening creatures could fetch a high price.

Thus, we headed for the woods near the village, on the hunt for such profitable monsters.

"H-hey, Megumin... Are we sure about this...? I know Bukkororii is with us, but if we get attacked by a bunch of enemies at once..."

"Oh, I suspect it will be fine. This NEET has the kind of time on his hands that only a NEET could have, and I think he spends quite a bit of it in this forest hunting for experience and pocket change."

"Quit it with the NEET business already. Even unemployed losers have human rights, okay? ...Gotta say, I'm not seeing any monsters, though. I guess it's because I went around with other people with time to kill and finished off all the big ones the other day so that you guys could have your combat practice... Oh, there's one, finally!"

Bukkororii, walking at the head of our line, lowered his voice. He was looking at a black creature digging up a tree root. It was a One-Punch Bear: a monster whose powerful forelimbs could take off a man's head with a single swipe.

"A One-Punch Bear, eh?" Bukkororii said. "Their livers are supposed to go for a lot of money... Perfect." He started chanting a spell, and then... "*Light of Reflection*."

The magic activated. At the same moment, Bukkororii, who had been walking just ahead of us, vanished. His spell must have bent the light to make him invisible. We could see his footprints advancing through the grass, so even though we couldn't see him, we knew he was getting closer to the monster.

The bear stood up, sniffing the air.

And then...

...it looked straight at us.

""Huh?!""

Yunyun and I thought we had been well hidden, but suddenly we were locking eyes with a monster. It gave a joyful roar at discovering fresh prey and charged at us.

"Yunyun, your dagger...! You must be carrying your dagger! Yunyun, my awesome rival, fight for me now!"

"Don't start calling me your rival all of a sudden just because you need a little help! Anyway, I can't possibly fight off a bear with nothing but a knife!"

The thought of running away crossed our minds, but the monster was shockingly fast!

And Bukkororii! Where was Bukkororii?!

"Where is that damn NEET hiding?! Bukkororii, hurry up and kill this thing!"

"Ahhhh, i-i-i-it's coming this waaaaaaaaayyy!"

The One-Punch Bear was practically on top of us.

"*Light of Saber!*"

Bukkororii suddenly appeared out of thin air, shouting and waving his hand. A beam of light followed the slicing motion of his arm. That beam, in fact, passed straight through the One-Punch Bear, which had never even turned around.

The light ran from the bear's shoulder down across its belly. It kept coming at us for another couple of seconds, then fell clean in two.

"Phew… Usually they just look around a little, even if they notice my scent. They're not usually so interested… So what did you both think? How was that for timing? If Soketto was in danger, I could jump out and save her right about th— Eeeyowch! H-hey, wait! I'm sorry! But what Crimson Magic Clansman wouldn't want to pick the perfect moment…?!"

Yunyun and I just kept punching him on the shoulders.

"Listen, kids, we don't have time to play around. If we don't do something about this dead monster, other creatures are going to smell the blood and come running." Bukkororii dusted himself off as he picked himself up from the ground.

"I don't believe you have the authority to say that, seeing as you're the reason we're angry in the first place. Grab that bear's liver and let's go home."

Sometimes when groups of Crimson Magic Clan members went hunting together, they deliberately left a body exposed in order to attract more prey. We, however, had only one NEET layabout to fight for us…

"Hey…" Yunyun tugged on my sleeve. I looked at her to discover her staring at something directly behind me, her face pale.

And then…

"L-l-l-look…" She pointed with a trembling finger.

Feeling distinctly uneasy, I turned around, and…!

"Let's get out of here! Bukkororii, forget about the liver! Your plan failed!"

"Eeeeyikes, wait for meeeee!"

""""*Grrrahhhh!*"""""

There was a whole pack of One-Punch Bears behind us, and they weren't happy about what we'd done to their friend!

4

"Now then, Yunyun. Shall we go home for lunch by-and-by?"

"I certainly think so. Well, I'll see you at school tomorrow, then."

"Wait! Don't abandon me! I'm begging youuu…!"

We had run all the way to the village, and now Bukkororii was tearfully trying to stop us from just going home. He was covered in mud from his attempts to draw off the rest of the bears.

I had to admit, the sight of a snotty, mud-spattered NEET prostrating himself in the dirt in front of us was enough to evoke anyone's sympathy, but…

"…*Sigh.* Very well. Just please be a mature adult and don't bow down to students. We can spare a few more minutes for you… Still, I wonder what we should do. How do we proceed with our plan to get to know Bukkororii's potential love interest…?"

"I've got a different question," Bukkororii said dejectedly. "Why were those One-Punch Bears even there? They don't normally form packs…"

"My dad said things have been strange in the forest lately. I wonder if it has something to do with why the monsters are behaving so unusually," Yunyun said—but there was no way for any of us to know.

"In any event," I started, "we will achieve nothing standing around here. Shall we go back to Soketto's shop?"

Thus, we headed back to our starting point, but…

"…The sign says she's gone out. I wonder where Soketto could be," Yunyun said.

We felt Bukkororii put a hand on each of our shoulders…

Let me tell you about Soketto, I can tell you because **Soketto and I are so close**, see? Soketto **wakes up at seven in the morning**, that's a great, healthy habit, and after she puts her sheets in the hamper, she starts making breakfast, which is **udon every single morning**, so I'm like, does she like udon that much? And while she's waiting for the water to boil, she **brushes her teeth** and **washes her face**, that's really efficient, don't you think, like, she's as **pretty** as she is **smart**, and **Soketto is really, really smart**. After she eats her udon, Soketto washes the breakfast dishes and the dishes from last night's dinner at the same time, see, so she can **let the dinner utensils soak overnight** every night because she is so smart, and I'm sure she'll make someone a great wife someday, and then Soketto takes a bath—she takes **a bath first thing in the morning**, she must really love to be clean, because **she takes one at night, too**, and that must be why she has such nice skin, and then when she gets out of the bath, she puts her clothes in the hamper and then, and **listen up, because this is the important part**, then **she does the laundry right away**, which is a real problem for me because—well, uh, no, it's not really a problem, it's just—it's no problem, because **I never do anything creepy**, and then after she does the laundry, Soketto takes a little **walk**, which is really healthy, huh? And after walking around a bit, she comes back to the shop, and you girls know what happens after that, how she starts by **cleaning**—she must really love to be clean, in fact she seems really good at all kinds of housework—and then after some cleaning, she goes back in the shop and doesn't come out again, which is too bad, plus I'm sure she must be bored in there, seriously, if I had the money, I would go there every single day, then after that if there are no customers maybe she gets bored, because she comes out and does a little light **stretching** and **peeks this way and that** like, *Are there gonna be any customers today?* and it's just adorable, it's totally against the rules the way she's not just **pretty** but **cute**, too, **have you seen how cute Soketto is?** And then she closes the shop and goes off somewhere, just leaves the store, and I love how she's **lackadaisical** like that, like some people might say she was being too **free**, but after all, I'm **a NEET who's always propounding freedom** and I think that would make us **perfect for each other**, and so but anyway, by now I think we've got **about two more hours** until she comes back, and I don't mind waiting, but what about you, what do you want to do?

Bukkororii performed this info dump with his eyes sparkling.

"Y-you sound like you're watching her every waking moment; it's most unsettling... How come you know so much about Soketto?"

"Aww, I just come here to check things out whenever I have a few minutes to spare. And not to brag, but I have the *most* minutes to spare of anyone in the village."

That really *wasn't* anything to brag about.

But wait...

"Y-you're just a stalk—"

"Careful, Yunyun. You may be the chief's daughter, but I won't let even you finish that thought."

If I attacked from behind, we might be able to bury him right here and now. It might be for the best.

"In any event, without Soketto, there is nothing for us to do here. I believe we should call it a day..."

Yunyun nodded emphatically.

"Don't worry—I think I know where she went," Bukkororii assured us with confidence.

"Well, I'll be. You were right."

"Yeah..."

I wasn't sure whether to be glad we had found Soketto or to report Bukkororii to the police.

Bukkororii had led us, mixed emotions and all, to the general store, where we found Soketto looking at the items for sale at the front.

"See? I can come through when it counts. Finding out where she goes when she leaves the store? Child's play."

Staaaalllkeeerrr...

"...Whatever. This time she's outside, so it will be less suspicious if we stop to talk to her. Yunyun and I will try to ask casually about her type. Let's go, Yunyun. I need someone to help gin up a conversation."

"Okay. Let's just ask and get this all over with."

Yunyun, looking immeasurably tired, went into the general store with me.

"Oh, Yunyun," I said. "Look at this. Is it not adorable?"

"Y-yeah, it's so cute! I'm sure if you gave it to the person you liked, he would... Huh?! W-were you talking about this thing?! It's a wooden sword with a dragon carved in it!"

Whereas I had found the perfect conversation starter, Yunyun had to go and mess it up.

"*Yunyun,*" I snarled under my voice, "*I need you to play along!*"

"*But you have the weirdest tastes, Megumin! How am I supposed to play along with that?*"

As we had a whispered argument, Soketto turned to us. "Oh my, isn't that cute? The dragon carving is wonderful! I think it would look great on you, hanging from your hip as you went around town."

"What?!" Yunyun almost choked.

"I completely agree. It combines practicality and adorability... Incidentally, Soketto. I wish to ask completely casually, what is your t—? Wh-what are you doing, Yunyun?!"

I had been just about to imperceptibly shift the topic to Soketto's preferred type when Yunyun grabbed my arm and interrupted me.

"*There was nothing casual about that! And what am I, crazy?! Am I the crazy one here?! There's no way anyone could consider that sword cute!*"

"*You have always been crazy, Yunyun, such as how you gave my cat the bizarre name Ink... Yipes!*"

As we resumed our whisper fighting, Soketto finished shopping and left the store.

"How could you have done that? Things were going perfectly!"

"But—! But—!!"

Now we were just fighting—we no longer had to whisper—when along came Bukkororii.

"What the hell are you two doing? Soketto just left!"

"Do not blame me; I was just about to strike the coup de grâce

when I was rudely interrupted… And another thing: How can someone who walks around armed with a dagger every day possibly dislike a wooden sword? But enough talk—we must be off!"

"My fashionable dagger is nothing like that piece of timber!"

"Can you please fight *later*?!"

Soketto was walking just ahead of us, in high spirits, holding the wooden sword she had earlier judged to be cute.

"…Ah, Soketto, walking along swinging a wooden sword. That mischievous side of her is so sweet…"

"I think everything about her screams *dangerous*," Yunyun whispered back to Bukkororii.

I listened to them with one ear as I watched Soketto swing her sword.

We were able to follow her thanks to Bukkororii's magic, which made us impossible to see.

"She certainly seems to like that sword. Look, she is slashing up falling leaves. I wonder if she thinks she is doing some sort of training?"

Completely unaware of us, Soketto bashed the tree trunk with her sword to shake off more dead leaves and gave it a few solid kicks.

"U-um, so what exactly is it that has you so enamored with Soketto? Are you really sure you want someone who goes around kicking tree trunks, Bukkororii?"

"Maybe it's her face. I really fell in love with her looks. And when a woman is beautiful enough, everything she does becomes sweet and adorable."

Bukkororii answered without hesitation, indeed, with alacrity, leaving Yunyun dumbstruck.

"Bukkororii," I said, following a sudden thought. "What if you were to just 'happen by' at some opportune moment when you could give Soketto some help? Say you use wind magic on that tree to bring the leaves down and then aid her in her training?"

"That's brilliant! That's the number one genius of the Crimson Magic Clan for you! Way to go, Megumin!"

"Oh! I—I can think of ways for you to get girls to like you, too, Bukkororii! Like, uh, fix your bedhead and get a job before you…"

Yunyun's sense of rivalship was burning hot, but Bukkororii paid no attention to her as he snuck a little closer to Soketto, still invisible.

Then…!

"*Tornado!*"

The whirlwind Bukkororii summoned sent Soketto high into the sky—

"He's a complete idiot! Isn't he a complete idiot?!"

"Let's bury him. Let's bury this NEET here and now!"

After making sure Soketto was safe, the three of us beat a hasty retreat, and now two of us were choking the life out of the third.

"Wait, please! Both of you need to just calm down! And be quieter! We don't want anyone to find us!"

Soketto, her face obviously white even from a distance, had managed to use wind magic on herself to regain her balance and get safely to the ground. Then she'd looked around, her red eyes clearly searching for the criminal who had cast the spell on her. But we were protected by Bukkororii's light-bending magic, so as long as we could keep quiet, she wouldn't find us.

That was when Yunyun had grabbed Bukkororii by the front of the shirt and demanded in a scrupulously quiet voice, "I thought you liked Soketto! So why would you attack her with a spell that could have killed her?!"

"Y-you've got it all wrong! Advanced magic is the only magic I know, so I can't go easy…! And I was just going to blow some leaves off the trees at first! But then I realized, if I used wind magic, her skirt might…"

"Let's bury him."

"I agree. Let's bury him alive."

"Wait! I'm begging you—hear me out!"

While we were fooling around, Soketto turned away with a look of disappointment on her face. Apparently, she had given up the hunt for her attacker.

"Phew... The important thing is that she's safe. And...at least I learned her favorite color."

Yunyun and I exclaimed: ""Sokettoooo!""

"S-s-s-stop that!"

5

At last it was time for lunch. I was going to hurry home to eat with Komekko, but...

"*Please* wait! *Please* don't abandon me!"

I would do the laundry that had been piling up, and then Komekko and I could play a game or something...

"Please, *please* don't ignore me! You're terrible! After I worked so hard to shake Soketto! She nearly saw me!"

Then we could have a bath. Maybe I could give the fur ball a bath, too...

"Pleeeeeeeease! I'm beeeeegging you! Ahhhhhh!"

"Will you be quiet?! Stop following us! Or do you intend to add us to your list of stalking targets? Just give up already and find someone else to fall in love with."

"Megumin is right; I think it's time for you to quit... Say, I've heard there's a cute monster called a Leisure Girl that lives near the village."

"And why would you tell me that?! Are you saying a monster is the best I can hope for?! How can you say that with such a straight face?"

Yunyun and I were trying to go home, but the stalker came around in front of us to cut off our escape. He had been like this ever since he had finally dodged Soketto.

"…Yeesh. It doesn't matter how many times you beg us—it won't work. We aren't made of free time. Unlike certain NEETs, us students have a hard life."

"I can help! Let me treat you to lunch!" Bukkororii suggested, bowing his head and putting his hands together in supplication.

"We're not kids; we can't be bought off so easily. Can we, Megumin…? Huh?"

She seemed surprised to find me happily following Bukkororii.

"Let us discuss battle plans while filling our bellies," I said.

"How can you live with yourself, Megumin?! …H-hey, I'll help, too; don't just leave me here!"

We were at the only café in town.

"I believe the key is to set up your meet-cute," I said around a mouthful of lambwich.

Bukkororii was watching Yunyun and me eat with a hungry expression on his face. It seemed our meals had finally consumed the last of his money.

""The key?""

"Correct. You have absolutely no connections with Soketto right now, yes? So first, allow Yunyun and me to create an opportunity for the two of you to get to know each other. The best-case scenario would of course be for you to go to her shop regularly and become friends, but that's obviously untenable in your current unemployed state. But we can at least work something out to get you two face-to-face."

"R-right!"

"Uh, how are we going to do that? Do you have any ideas?" Yunyun asked.

I sipped the last of my juice and replied, "It couldn't be simpler. First, Yunyun, you put on a mask or something, then take your dagger and attack Soketto. Bukkororii happens to be walking by, and—"

"That's brilliant!"

"No way! Are you completely stupid?! You must be completely stupid!"

The café owner, who couldn't help overhearing our high-volume conversation, commented, "I keep hearing Soketto's name come up... Do you need something with her? She's in the forest with her wooden sword."

"No, nothing in particu— *Forest?!*"

Yunyun and I looked at each other.

Bukkororii may or may not have understood what we were thinking, but he said proudly...

The forest? So Soketto went into the forest! **She does that every day** because **she loves training**, so she goes into the woods **to hunt monsters**, and her favorite monster to hunt is the Fire Drake, and what she likes to do is freeze them and then laugh at them, and you know what? She and I **totally have that in common**, like, I'm a NEET, right? So I've got lots of time on my hands, and so sometimes I get some ice, right? I make some ice and then just watch it meeeelt the whole entire day, and I'm sure Soketto's the same way, or maybe not? Anyway, who cares, the point is, Soketto **goes to the woods to train every day**, and her fighting style is **super amazing**, see, because she likes **lightning magic**, and lightning is pretty just like she is, so they go together perfectly, sorry about that, I got off subject, but anyway, I'm sure **she's in the woods training right now**, and did you know her level is gonna be **50** soon, which is incredible, there aren't that many Level 50s even in the Crimson Magic Clan, she's like a number one top-class adventurer, Soketto is, so she's **pretty** and **cute** and **strong**, too, and that's totally unfair, and Soketto is so gorgeous when she's fighting, but then after she's done fighting, I just feel it **right here**, you know, because the **sweat** gets on her **beautiful black hair** and **white cheeks** and that **nape**, and it's totally unfair, it's against the rules, can you blame me for being **totally hot** for her? She should **take a little responsibility for crying out loud** but anyway that doesn't matter, I mean it does, but right now it doesn't, because **the point is she's totally definitely in the woods for training right now**, I'm sure she's chasing down a One-Punch Bear and going *Ah-ha-ha-ha-ha* or freezing a Fire Drake's feet and just having a grand old time, it would be great to see it, don't you want to see it, let's go see it, yeah, let's go see Soketto laughing and fighting and we can all fall in love with her together yeah let's!

"You are not making a strong case for not being creepy. How do you even know those things? But more importantly…! Remember how the One-Punch Bears formed a pack when we were in the woods earlier? The monsters have been acting strange recently. And Soketto is wandering right toward them…"

"W-w-wait, is she going to be okay?! We know people have seen strange monsters around here. Maybe we should call someone?"

Bukkororii interrupted Yunyun and me, however, with a small whisper. "I have to go to her…"

He sounded like a hero who had discovered his heroine was in danger.

"B-Bukkororii…?"

Yunyun watched him, worried, as he stood up with a deeply serious expression. "I'm heading to the woods right now! I have to find Soketto…!"

Yunyun's face suddenly lit up. "Th-that's it! The way you look now, Bukkororii, you're almost…!" She clenched her fist, overcome with emotion.

"Soketto might have run into that same group of bears…! What if I showed up and awesomely saved her? Right when she really needed me? You think she might ask me to make love to her right then and there?! …Er, Yunyun, were you saying something?"

"No, I was just thinking how nice it would be if you got eaten by a One-Punch Bear."

6

When we got to the woods, it looked different from before.

"…What's this? It looks like there's already been a major battle."

We were only just near the entrance, but it was obvious someone had been fighting. The trees nearby were scorched, maybe from fire or lightning magic. And smack in the middle of the circle of blackened vegetation was the corpse of a One-Punch Bear, smoke rising from its head.

"You can still smell the ozone. Whoever did this can't be far away," Bukkororii declared, scanning the area alertly.

"I have to wonder if a couple of ball and chains like me and Yunyun should even be here. If a One-Punch Bear does show up, we won't be able to do anything but scream and run away."

"Yeah. Honestly, I really want to go home now…"

"What are you talking about? If I ran into Soketto right now, I wouldn't have any way to start a conversation with her. Not to brag, but my mouth stops functioning when I'm confronted with a woman my age."

"What good does it do you to bring up your communication difficulties? Yunyun, back me up on this… Yunyun?"

"Hrk?! Wh-what?"

Yunyun had frozen in place, and her eyes had gotten strangely full at the words *communication difficulties.*

…Apparently, Bukkororii wasn't the only one who had them.

That was when we saw it.

"…Lightning magic?"

A bolt had fallen from the blue not far away from us…

"Lightning Strike!"

I thought I saw the sky light up at the powerful voice. And then, an instant later, a bolt of lightning came crashing among the trees.

The One-Punch Bear who took the hit fell to the ground, smoking from the head. Maybe it was animal instinct that caused the rest of the pack to stop in their tracks at the stupendous clap of thunder.

Standing in the middle of the crowd of bears was a young woman with red eyes. It was Soketto, wooden sword in hand, eyes blazing, looking downright thrilled as she intoned her magic.

"Lightning Strike!"

This must have been what had charred those trees.

At Soketto's shout, another blast of lightning came down on another of the immobilized One-Punch Bears. As the second monster fell, Bukkororii went running in. He didn't look like his usual NEET self. Instead, he looked like a member of the Crimson Magic Clan racing to protect someone he loved.

Eyes blazing red, Bukkororii cast his spell as a veritable shout. The recognition of a new enemy, us, sent the bears into action again.

"Purifying flames of hell! Rage and burn! *Inferno*!" He invoked the most powerful fire magic with all his strength…

…and caught Soketto in the blast.

"S-S-Sokettoooo!" Yunyun exclaimed.

"What are you doing, you idiotic NEET? Quick! We have to do something to help, or…?!"

The pack of One-Punch Bears was going up in flames, along with the entire forest. But Soketto walked toward us, her body surrounded by a thin membrane of water. It looked like she had managed to cast a protective water spell on herself.

"Y-you're safe! Thank goodness…!"

"No kidding! I thought my heart was going to stop…! Bukkororii, do something about this fire! The entire forest is going to burn down!"

My command induced Bukkororii to hurriedly douse the flames with water magic. He might have been a no-account NEET, but he was, after all, also a member of the Crimson Magic Clan who knew advanced magic.

Bukkororii's wholesale blast of fire magic had incinerated the One-Punch Bears. Parts of the forest were still burning here and there. Soketto, meanwhile, had let down her bubble of water and turned brimming eyes on Bukkororii. Was that because of the battle, or was there something else at work? Soketto's cheeks were red, and she seemed lost for words.

Bukkororii, looking nervous, stood in front of her, his face just as red. But after actually looking a little bit cool, the NEET dropped the ball when it counted. Sheer nervousness prevented him from coming up with anything to say.

"…I believe Bukkororii has something to tell you," I offered.

""""?!""" The other three there caught their collective breath.

Yunyun was watching the progress of the conversation, her face flushed.

Bukkororii was panicking because he didn't know what to do.

And Soketto?

"Isn't that funny, Bukkororii. There's something I want to say to you, too."

Yunyun, Bukkororii, and I all goggled at this most unexpected pronouncement.

"W-w-well…! Could it be that you…?!"

"That's right. I'm sure I feel the same way you do." A soft smile came over Soketto's face. Bukkororii turned as red as a tomato to be graced with such a sweet expression.

Was it because he had saved her? I had heard of the so-called suspension-bridge effect, where you fall in love with someone because you're scared… Could it be that?

The laziest NEET layabout in town winning the heart of the village's most beautiful girl? I couldn't quite believe it, but when I saw Yunyun with her cheeks red and her eyes shining, I started to think maybe all was well that ended well.

Bukkororii found his courage, clenched his fist, and said… "S-Soketto, I've always—!"

"You should have just *told* me you hated me. This forest is the perfect place. I hear you come here all the time to train, just like I do. I think you'll be the perfect opponent…so let's have our climactic final showdown right here and now!"

………

""""Huh?"""""

Everyone but Soketto sounded very confused.

"I don't know what it is you loathe so much about me! And I've seen you tailing me before, but today was different! First you try to kill me right in the middle of town with Tornado, then you ambush me with Inferno when I'm surrounded by monsters and can't defend myself…! Heh, you really know how to make your move. I've faced a lot of monsters in my time, but you're the only one who's ever had me on the ropes like this!" The wooden sword in Soketto's hand made a creaking sound.

"N-n-n-n-n-no! That's not true; you've got it all wrong! I was trying to *save* you from those monsters with that spell…! I'm really sorry for catching you in it; I was just so bent on helping!"

At the sight of Bukkororii, pale-faced and waving his hands, Soketto's grip on her sword loosened. "…So how do you explain that Tornado earlier, then? You tried to hide, but I know it was you. You're the only one who would follow me around like that."

"That, uh, it…!" Bukkororii looked to us for help.

Yunyun and I pointed at him. ""He said he was trying to see up your skirt.""

That was when Soketto went after Bukkororii with her sword.

7

We were in a shop bedecked with light-purple drapes. Soketto looked at us with disappointment. "I'm sure this hasn't been much easier for you two than it has for me. I'm assuming that perv dragged you into this?"

We had come back from the forest and settled in Soketto's shop.

"Stop with the perv stuff already, please. I didn't do it for any, like, creepy reason. I just wondered what Crimson Magic Clan girls' favorite color was. You know, just a wizard's desire to learn about the world around h— I'm sorry! Yes, I did it because I'm a bad guy. Please just put down the sword!"

When Soketto went for the wooden blade resting against the wall, Bukkororii, who was in the process of being wrapped with bandages, quickly backed down. After a fairly thorough beating at Soketto's hands, he was now receiving Yunyun's ministrations.

Soketto heaved a sigh. "…Geez. If you wanted to have your fortune told so badly that you were willing to go into the woods to earn money, you should have talked to me. I can comp you at least the first time."

"Really?!"

In the end, our chicken NEET never admitted the real reason he had been in the woods. Instead, he had claimed that he wanted to know something about his future and had been saving up the money for a fortune-telling. He had just happened to come across Soketto and the monsters and had stopped to help.

"We'll call the Tornado an exception, and you did try to help me in the woods, even if you almost burned me to a crisp doing it. I guess I could tell your fortune one time… So what is it you want to know?"

Soketto produced a crystal ball from the back of the shop and set it in front of Bukkororii.

"I w-want to…to know about my future g-girlfriend—I mean wife—no, no, maybe the person who'll fall in love with me? …Argh, which do I pick?!"

Bukkororii was suddenly in danger of forgetting why he was here. That was clearly obvious to Soketto, who grabbed the crystal ball with an expression of annoyance. "You want to know about your future in love; that's what you're saying, right? Look into the crystal ball, and you will see the woman you're most likely to be involved with in the future. The future can be changed, though. So I'm not saying she's The One for sure… Ooh, you'll see her soon…!"

A pale glow began to emanate from Soketto's crystal ball. A moment later, it faded again, and…!

"…I, uh, can't see anything."

"What, really?!" Soketto, who had maintained her composure even when being tossed into the air by a tornado, looked downright shocked and gave the crystal ball a hearty shake. "J-just a second. What's going on? It's never... Everyone ought to see at least *one* person...!"

"Maybe wait until you're out of earshot to say something that's going to cut that deep," he suggested.

The fact that Bukkororii didn't see anyone suggested that he certainly had no chance with Soketto. She looked at him with pity when she saw his eyes fill with tears. "...Look, it's okay. My fortunes aren't always right... There was a time I tried to predict the weather as a girl, and when I said it would be cloudy, there was a five-minute downpour instead..."

"Please stop! I can't even tell if you're being nice or bragging about how accurate your predictions are! Argh, this is *so much worse* than just being shot down!"

Yunyun and I gave them some space and started whispering to each other.

"I feel bad watching this happen to anyone, even that NEET. If he didn't see *anyone*, that means even the female monsters like the Leisure Girl you joked about won't take him..."

"What do we do? I never thought it would be this bad..."

"I can hear you! If you have to talk about me, please do it more quietly!"

Bukkororii left the place nearly in tears.

"Come to think of it, he explained his way out of the two incidents today, but he got so upset over that fortune that I completely forgot to ask him why he follows me around all the *rest* of the time."

"Er... I wouldn't bring it up. For both your sakes."

Soketto cocked her head in puzzlement. She watched Bukkororii go away to nurse his aching body and heart. "He may be completely useless, but he seems interesting, too. It's strange..." Soketto turned the crystal ball over in her palm.

8

We were on the way home from Soketto's shop.

"I guess it didn't work out, huh?" Yunyun observed. "Maybe Bukkororii should think about finding a job first…"

"Maybe Bukkororii should think about knowing a lost cause when he sees one. He lives near me and I have known him my entire life, and I can tell you he is completely hopeless."

Yunyun glanced over at me. "Oh yeah, he's been sort of like an older brother to you, hasn't he, Megumin? …L-like a childhood friend, right? It would be totally natural for you to develop feelings for—"

"Nope."

Yunyun looked almost hopeful, but I shot her down.

"O-oh… I keep wondering, Megumin, is food really the only thing on your mind? Don't you ever think you would want to fall in love with a wonderful person or something?"

"There is something I must do," I said firmly, "and I do not have time for puppy love."

Yunyun, however, refused to give up. "B-but you plan on becoming an adventurer someday, don't you? And that means sleeping and eating with your party members all the time, helping them and being helped…!"

"I have indeed heard that marriages between party members are frequent… But, well, I just don't see it happening in my case."

"You sound so sure. I have to admit, I can't really picture you mooning over someone, following them around…"

As we chatted, we arrived at my house.

"In any event, *were* I ever to fall in love…I'm sure it would be with only the coolest, most awesome person I could find."

"Gosh, I always figured you would marry someone who was just average…"

*   *   *

I said good-bye to Yunyun, then went inside…

"I'm home!"

"Welcome back, Sis!"

Komekko came bounding in, holding Ink. The cat's head was drooping in exhaustion; I was sure she had been pressed into being Komekko's playmate while I was gone.

"Sis, let's eat! There's lots of delicious stuff!"

…*Lots of delicious stuff?*

"Whatever do you mean? Did someone give you food again?"

"Bukkororii brought it by. He said to make sure I grow up nice and beautiful, and then he'll be happy to make me his br—"

Before she had finished, I was already racing out the door to the cobbler's place to give that boy a beatdown.

Slyest Demon of the Little Sisters of the Crimson Magic Clan

I solved the second puzzle.

"…I really hate the Crimson Magic Clan."

"*I'm* part of the Crimson Magic Clan."

"………Well, I hate all of them except you." A third puzzle had emerged from the pedestal just when Host and I had thought we were done. Host paused. "Arrrgh, forget it. This is way too tough for me. Heck, I think even you might not be up to this one. This puzzle's not for kids."

"My big sister told me that doing the impossible is what Crimson Magic Clan members live for."

And then I lay down on the ground, kicking my feet, and worked on the puzzle.

"Hey, don't you have any manners? Your shoes are covered in mud. Blargh…"

Host was busy trying to clean my robe, but I was focused on the puzzle.

"…Whoa, hey, you're killin' that thing! I think this might just work! Hey, what's wrong? Did it get hard all of a sudden?"

Halfway through the puzzle, I had put my head down and closed my eyes. "Bored now."

"Aww, sweet li'l Komekko, I'm beggin' ya! You can't quit now! Is it food you want?! You must be hungry! The Great Lord Host'll scare something up for you!"

At that, I sat up and started working on the puzzle again.

"G-great! You just keep at it! I'll find something for you quick!" Host spread his wings and was just about to launch himself into the sky.

"Ooh! Take me! I wanna go, too!"

"N-no way, kiddo! I'm not taking a shrimp like you into the woods! The monsters in there would eat you alive!"

"But I wanna! I wanna go! Host, you look so strong, I'm sure I'd be fine!"

"Well, uh, I sure am strong! I mean, I send those monsters running just by showing up in the woods!"

"You're so cool, Lord Host!"

And so he took me along.

"*Huff... Puff...* You're out of control, kid; slow down already!"

"Look, it's a big ol' lizard! That one, Host! Catch that lizard!"

"Listen to me, will ya?!"

Host had carried me over to the forest.

"Aww, look, Komekko. He ran away because of all your shouting. When you're as big and bad a demon as I am, everyone knows it, and they don't stick around. I've been coming here every so often to catch your snacks. Maybe I can head back to the entrance to the woods and find all the monsters who have been trying to run away."

"...When I get big and strong, will the monsters run away from me?"

"Huh, I dunno about that! No matter how strong you get, I don't know if any monster would run away from a pip-squeak like you! Hee-hee-ha-ha!"

Host set me down, laughing. I saw the bushes shaking just ahead of us.

"Oh? Something that ain't gonna run away when it notices me? Here comes something with some guts."

"Ooh, so if I can get that monster to run away, does that mean I'm stronger than you, Host?"

"Buh! O-oh, snap, didn't mean to spit! Heh-heh, yeah, I guess that's what it'd mean. But there's a big, scaaary monster in those bushes, see? When you get a look at it, don't go wettin' your pants, eh?"

"I won't wet nothing! I'll chase it off!"

That only made Host laugh harder. "I'd like to see you try! Go on—give it hell! If you really chase it off, I'll call you Komekko the Great for the rest of my life."

Then a big bear came jumping out of the bushes.

"...Huh, a One-Punch Bear. A whole pack of 'em. Y'know, I think this is too much, even for us. All right, you ugly mugs, I'll let y' off this time..." Host turned around.

But as for me, I went running straight toward them. "Kishaaaaa!"

"Lady Komekko?!" shouted Host as he dived into the pack after me.

Chapter
4

What Sleeps in
Crimson Magic
Village

1

Heartbroken, Bukkororii had shut himself up in his house for the past three days.

Otherwise, things were pretty uneventful. But...

I couldn't help feeling Yunyun was acting a little strange lately.

"Good morning, Megumin. Here, this is for you." She handed me a lunch box as I walked into the classroom.

It was so sudden, I wasn't sure how to react. Finally, standing there with the gift in my hands, I said, "What is this? Have you perhaps fallen in love with me? To abruptly have someone preparing meals for me like a devoted wife is somewhat..."

"Devoted wife?! What are you talking about?! I didn't feel like challenging you today, so I decided to just give you something to eat! You've got your food now, so don't bother me!"

...*Pfft.*

"Why, anyone listening to you would think I was some common

bandit who scrounged my sustenance from you whenever I couldn't get a bite to eat."

"I know it's partly my fault for challenging you every day, but you *are* a bandit."

I was trying to decide what to do about this remarkably assertive answer from Yunyun when the teacher came into the room. The chatter among the students quieted as he stood at the lectern.

"Good morning," he said. "Monsters like the one that appeared during our recent lesson, presumably servants of the Dark God, have been sighted around town. We can't afford to sit on our hands now."

That set the class buzzing again.

Most monsters less powerful than the likes of a One-Punch Bear fled the moment they so much as laid eyes on a member of the Crimson Magic Clan. If some monsters were actually entering the village, that truly was unusual.

"Therefore, we've decided to forcibly reseal the Dark God, although we're still getting our people together. The ritual will begin tomorrow evening and last through the night. In the unlikely event that we fail, the deity's servants may flood the town. We have safety measures in place just in case that happens, but I urge you not to leave your houses after the ritual begins."

Our teacher, usually so disinterested, looked uncharacteristically serious. I hadn't been paying that much attention to the goings-on in the village, but it looked like things were turning grim.

"All right. With that out of the way, let's move on to the results of the other day's test. As usual, the top three scorers will receive a skill-up potion! Come to the front of the class when I call your name! ...Third, Nerimaki!"

I listened to the teacher with one ear and looked at my Adventurer's Card.

Heh-heh-heh, another four points.

With just four more points, I could learn the Explosion spell I so craved.

"Second, Arue!"

I listened to the teacher with one ear and grinned at my Adventurer's Card.

...*Arue second?*

"And number one, Megumin! Good work. Come get your potion."

As I stood, I glanced over at Yunyun. Yunyun, who was sitting there with her fists clenched, looking somehow nervous.

"First period is going to be Cool-Item Creation. You'll be making statement pieces that display your individuality, like Arue's eye patch. If you're not sure what to make, I recommend bandannas or fingerless gloves. Everyone head to the home-economics room. I'll see you there!"

As the teacher left the room, I went back to my seat, inching closer to Yunyun to make sure she could see my newly acquired potion. She looked away, annoyed, and I gave the potion a shake, making a *splish-splish* sound.

Yunyun finally caved, pounding her desk as she stood up. "...Why don't you say something?! It really bugs me when you just parade around like that!"

Somehow, though, her anger lacked its usual bite.

"...Then, indeed, I shall say something. Your only good qualities, Yunyun, are that you are a skilled cook, an excellent student, and you have no real personal presence. What in the world happened this time?"

"Hey, I'm not sure that last one is actually a good thing! What do you mean, I have no presence?! And anyway, I'm sure I have more good qualities than that!" She was red-faced with her objections.

I thrust the potion toward her. "I know you said you weren't going to challenge me, but how about it? As I recall, Yunyun, you needed another three points to achieve Advanced Magic. And I need four points... Can you really accept that? You were ahead of me—*me*! And here it looked like you were going to graduate before me. How about it?"

My taunting produced a medley of emotions on Yunyun's face...

"I told you, n-no contests today... Go ahead and drink that potion."

"...I see. Well, so it goes. I'll have it along with this breakfast."

I drank the potion down and started in on my meal...and for some reason, Yunyun looked relieved.

I knew something's been wrong with that girl.

2

"Hey, have you heard? Have you heard the rumor that a hero candidate's coming to town?"

Our morning class was over, and Funifura had approached Yunyun and me, bringing her own lunch. She was the one who shared this information, looking very pleased about it.

Crimson Magic Village was just a rural burg—one surrounded by dangerous monsters. Why would a hero candidate come here?

A "hero candidate" was what people called the ones with bizarre names who had been gifted special powers by the gods. And their names weren't the only things that were strange. Word was that their behavior, personalities, and even their idea of common sense all cut against the grain.

"I know—I heard!" Dodonko said. "I even saw him yesterday! He's, like, cool *and* hot at the same time, and he said he's here to find some party members to help him defeat the Demon King! He wants a powerful wizard! Argh, why'd he have to come *now*? If only I knew some magic, I'd follow him in a second!" She sighed wistfully.

...Hmm. A hero candidate who is at once cool and hot?

I still was not able to use magic, so I wouldn't be joining anyone's party just yet...but a wizard with potential like mine might well run into a hero candidate like him someday.

Powerful chosen ones have a certain magnetism to attract their kin, after all. Birds of a feather, as they say.

Yunyun, her interest piqued, said, "A hero candidate, huh...? What was he like? Did he seem strong?"

"He had these two girls with him and a sword that gave off this huge magic aura. He seemed like a nice guy. He said he was a...Sword Master, I guess? His name was...Mitsu...ragi...?"

A Sword Master with a powerful magic sword? If he had made it through all the monsters living around our village, that was proof enough of his strength.

"I see," I noted. "And how long does this person intend to stay here? If it will be long enough for me to learn magic, I would certainly like to go with him."

Dodonko shook her head. "He said he'll be leaving today or tomorrow. And anyway, if he *did* stay, I would have dibs on him."

That was too bad. A hero candidate was almost guaranteed to be a fine specimen of humanity, a legendary hero type who could easily overcome any challenge. I hoped to join an adventuring party myself one day, and when I did, I would make sure it was with someone like that. Someone upstanding and righteous, willing and able to confront any crisis, the kind of hero candidate anyone and everyone would be infatuated with. And at his or her side, I would bring my magic to bear on every enemy, even a general of the Demon King, and make my fame resound throughout the world. And then I would defeat the Demon King and would myself be the new Demon King, Megumin—!

"Megumin, are you listening? What's with that smile? A-are you okay?"

"I was engaged in some very important thinking and did not hear you. What did you say?"

Yunyun brought me back to reality. Funifura and Dodonko were already happily chatting about something else. Yunyun kept one eye on them as she said apologetically to me, "Listen, Megumin. Could we walk home together? There's something I want to ask you about..."

3

School ended that day with nothing more unusual happening than Yunyun's failure to be one of our top scorers, and she and I headed home.

Even though she was the one who said she wanted to ask me about something, for a long time she didn't say anything at all. Finally, she opened her mouth.

"...Megumin, uh... Friends. What exactly are they supposed to be to each other...?"

I stopped cold and put a hand up to my eyes. This was a far more serious question than anything I had expected.

"H-hey, Megumin, what's wrong?! Hey, Megumin, I didn't make you cry, did I?! Hey!"

"No, I knew how pitifully lonely you are, Yunyun, but I never imagined it would go so deep that you don't even know what a friend is..."

"Of course I do! I know what a friend is! They go shopping and hang out together! But that's not what I'm asking!" Yunyun's anger passed, and she said more reservedly, "Megumin, you...you mooch off me all the time, but you never ask for money. Even if you do look at me like you want to be treated to a meal or come around staring longingly at my food at lunchtime."

"Of course. Even I know when I'm crossing the line. Besides, if I asked you for money, I could no longer say no even if you demanded my very body in return."

"I wouldn't demand that; what do you take me for?! Look, the point is, I thought friends didn't really ask each other for money. But...well, the other day, Funifura, she... I guess her little brother is really sick, and..."

I didn't know much about Funifura's family situation, but I was aware that she had a considerably younger brother whom she doted on.

"I guess she needs money to buy medicine for him, and I wondered if it would be rude to give her some money... Like, it's only natural to help a friend in need, but I wouldn't want her to get upset with me..."

"Did Funifura ask you to lend her money?"

Yunyun waved her hands emphatically. "Oh, n-no, she didn't, okay? She just said she needed money for medicine. But Dodonko immediately offered to help her out, and I was thinking maybe I should, too…"

Sheesh—I could see Yunyun was as gullible as ever.

I was becoming properly angry about the recent course of events. Those girls already had something of a poor reputation, and it had struck me as strange that they were suddenly such good friends with Yunyun. And then for Dodonko to offer money to Funifura right in front of Yunyun, as if to say, *This is what real friends do…*

The fact that she was talking to me about it meant Yunyun must have sensed something. But with no experience of friendship and a deep-seated fear of being disliked, it would be easy for her to get swept along.

"Personally," I offered, "I would find some other way to help her besides money. Part of the problem being that I have no money to give."

"Some other way…?"

"That's right… For example, cover your faces and lead your friends in robbing the drugstore."

"Wait, is that actually a better solution than just giving her money?!"

I wagged a finger at Yunyun. "Friends don't just wait for handouts; they suffer together, understand? Anyone can simply *give* something. Is it not much more meaningful to face a punishing challenge together?"

"So you mean when you're starving, rather than giving you lunch, I should starve with you?"

"……No, that is completely different, with no bearing on this… But look, you have to do something that makes sense to you. You cannot buy friendship with money, but I think sometimes you may give some of your hard-earned cash to a friend who is truly in need. Incidentally, I am truly in need at all times."

"I saw how you worked in something for yourself there," Yunyun said. "But I understand. Thanks, I'll figure out what to do."

…It didn't take me long to guess what this infinitely generous girl intended to do. And although I knew it wasn't quite aboveboard, I couldn't leave her to her own devices. If she was going to give Funifura money, she would most likely do it the next day before or after class. So, although it didn't technically have anything to do with me, the next day, I would…

Our talk subsided and we walked in silence for a while until we ran into Bukkororii.

"Oh, h-hi, Bukkororii!"

"Huh, Bukkororii, what are you doing here? I thought you were still locking yourself in your room after Soketto shot you down."

"Megumin! Hush!"

"Wrong! Considerately hushing her actually hurts me more! Anyway, I didn't confess, so I haven't been shot down!" As pathetic as that sounded, Bukkororii suddenly turned serious. "I get it now. I can't be messing around falling in love when the world awaits my awakening… People have been seeing those alleged servants of the Dark God everywhere. My power might be called on again, so I'm proactively patrolling the village just in case."

So, in other words, our NEET had recovered from his heartbreak and once again had too much time on his hands.

"Yes, I heard. I heard you and a handful of your NEET friends had formed some kind of vigilante group."

"Don't call it that. It has a name. An awesome name: the anti–Demon King wandering patrol, the Red-Eye Dead Slayers!"

Since the Demon King's army was too scared to come anywhere near our village, it wasn't clear to me why they were wandering or what they were patrolling for. They were just a group of Crimson Magic Clan folk with nothing but a name to boast about.

"The grown-ups do seem to be having a great deal of trouble with these monsters. Our teacher said they're going to try some kind of forcible resealing tomorrow. Why do all that? Why not simply free the deity and then eliminate it with the collective strength of the villagers?"

This was, after all, a village composed entirely of killer Arch-wizards. Even neighboring countries refused to negotiate with us. I couldn't imagine that our entire population together couldn't deal with one measly Dark God…

"Some people have suggested that. But the whole reason the Dark God is sealed up outside of town is apparently that our ancestors got it already sealed from somewhere else and brought it here."

"What?! I never knew that! Why?! Why would our ancestors do something so pointless that was so much trouble?!"

Bukkororii met the shouting Yunyun with a look of incomprehension. "Isn't it cool to be the place where the Dark God is sealed up? …So anyway, they want to seal it again. There aren't that many places that can claim to have a Dark God of their own. And we have plenty of experience with dangerous tourist attractions, like the weapon that could potentially destroy the entire world and the goddess of puppetry and revenge whose very name has been forgotten because all her followers have vanished."

"As much trouble as it's going to be, I have a certain interest in the forbidden weapon myself. I can understand how the village people feel."

"You can?! Wait, am I crazy?! Is there something wrong with me?!"

""Definitely.""

"Huh?!"

4

The next day.

I stuffed Ink into my bag and left for school earlier than usual. And on the way, just as I expected, I saw three familiar figures.

"Thanks, Yunyun! It's a big help! I'll be sure to thank you properly later, okay?"

"O-oh, you don't have to thank me! W-we're friends! U-um, let's just head to school together…"

It was Funifura, Dodonko, and Yunyun. Funifura had accepted something from Yunyun and flashed her an ingratiating smile.

"Oh… G-gee, I'm sorry. I have to take this over right away."

"Yeah, that's right, Funifura—if you don't hurry, your brother will… Anyway, Yunyun, how about you go on ahead?"

"Oh, uh, okay… I'm sorry. I wasn't thinking… I'll see you at school, then." She smiled at them and headed off to school on her own. As she walked away, her shoulders slumped, a pitiful sight if there ever was one.

Funifura and Dodonko watched her go for a moment, then said:

"It kind of…"

"…f-feels wrong, doesn't it…?"

"Heh-heh-heh… There's a simple cure for that: Don't do such things."

""?!""

The girls flinched as I spoke up from behind them.

"Megumin?! How long have you been there?!"

"Yeah, how long were you eavesdropping on our conversation with Yunyun?!"

I crawled out of the bushes where I had been hiding myself. "You want to know how much I heard? Well…"

Psst.
The next two pages reflect the original Japanese orientation, so read backward!

"…and then you told her that if she didn't want you to reveal her most embarrassing secrets, she had to do all the naughty things you told her to!"

"We did not! We did no such thing!"

"Why would we even do that?! Who do you think we are?"

My little joke had turned both their faces bright red.

"Look," Funifura said, "I just… I just borrowed a little money from Yunyun. The truth is, my little brother, he…"

"Yeah, that's right. Funifura's little brother is super sick, and he needs medicine. We couldn't come up with the money on our own, so we asked Yunyun."

"My, what a dire predicament… But how very aloof you are. If you were in such dire straits, you should have told me."

""Huh?!""

They were very surprised at my proclamation.

"What? Are you amazed that I would offer to help someone in need? Or are you trying to pick a fight with me?"

"W-we're not…! We're not picking a fight with anyone, but look. You… You're, like, super poor, aren't you?"

"Totally poor. No matter how badly we needed money, we could never come to you, Megumin."

"I'll kill you both." I started swinging my bag, ready to attack, but they both just frowned.

"S-so how did you think you were going to help us?"

"Yeah, that's right! You're so worked up about this, are you actually going to lend us money or something?!"

"I could never. Who do you think you're talking to? You must consider whom you are asking."

""Wh-why, you…!!""

Veins were bulging out of their foreheads, but I hadn't really been teasing them. "Now, now, calm down and listen. You want money for medicine. In that case, I need only bring you medicine, even if I have no money. Is that right?"

"Wha…? I mean, yeah, but…"

"Do you know how to get medicine?"

I gave them a knowing smile. "Just leave it to the greatest genius of the Crimson Magic Clan," I declared, full of confidence, but they just looked at each other, worried.

5

Hmm. Despite what I had said to the girls, I had no idea how to get medicine for them.

Maybe I could take Komekko to the drugstore and have her beg for some? She was so sly, it might just work.

"Ink! Hang in there, sweetie! What happened?! Why are you in such bad shape?! Megumin… Don't tell me you forgot Ink was in here and swung your bag around on the way to school?!"

In her seat beside mine, Yunyun was clutching Ink and making a huge fuss, but I let it wash over me. I tried to think of a way to craft a sickness-healing potion.

At length, our teacher came in, looking listless. We all took our seats, just as usual…

"*Ahem.* I believe I've told you that the resealing of the Dark God would take place tonight. I don't expect there'll be any problems, but you never know for sure. I've been saving a special something just in case the resealing fails, and I'll be waiting with it at the ready—though I hope I won't have to use it. And I doubt I will, since the projected success rate of the ceremony is better than ninety percent. Yes, I would certainly rather *not* have to use it…"

If there was a more obvious setup for failure, I did not know it.

I watched him—he seemed oddly fidgety—and started to wonder if in fact he *wanted* the ceremony to go wrong. Then he would have a chance to use this thing he seemed so intent on bragging about even though no one had asked him to elaborate.

"Anyway, on that note. Today you should go straight home, no detours. And once you get home, stay there for the night. Now, first period is Magical-Item Crafting. Everyone, head for the laboratory! Get going!"

Everyone started bustling out of the room…and that's when it hit me. *Magical item crafting…!*

The laboratory was situated beneath the school building. Was that because we were handling dangerous chemicals and potentially explosive substances? No. It was because the builders just figured an underground laboratory was the obvious place for a wizard to do their bizarre experiments.

We could sit in any open spot in the laboratory, but I was always in the front row.

The teacher came up to the lectern, scratching his head. "All right, we're going to get started on magical item crafting here. The creation of magical potions and items is an important source of income for us wizards, so it won't hurt you to pick it up. Now……Megumin, I like your attitude, but don't get too far ahead."

"I'm sorry, sir. This is my favorite class."

The teacher gestured at me to move back a little from my front-row spot, then picked up a bottle. "Now, I know we've been over the basics before, but they're important. Let's start with a simple healing potion and… Megumin, you have your hand up. Got a question?"

"Please skip these cheap consumables and teach us to make something harder and more lucrative, sir."

"All right, you'll be my assistant for this class. I'll work you like a dog, so you'll stop mewling like a kitten."

No fair!

I trudged around, helping the teacher as he went through his explanation.

"Okay, everyone pick your favorite ingredients and get to work on a potion. If you succeed, you can start adding some personal touches.

Remember, the proportions can change the potion's effect. Make something that's uniquely yours."

When I had finally finished passing out tools and materials to my classmates, my mind went back to my original objective. "Teacher," I started. "I have a question. Do you think I'm capable of creating a sickness-curing potion?"

"Something to cure illness? It's not impossible, but those aren't easy potions. And just so you know, the materials tend to be expensive, and they don't sell well. You aren't going to be making a profit on them, okay?"

"I understand how it is that you see me, sir. This is not about money but about helping someone I know who is ill. I'd hoped I could do something for them."

The teacher scratched his chin. "…If that's what you're after, then go ahead and use our materials. Here's a recipe—take it… Gosh, to think such a freewheeling, money-grubbing, totally-ruthless-and-able-to-kill-a-monster-without-hesitating person as you had a real heart."

"Now I really and truly understand how it is that you see me, sir."

Privately vowing to pay this teacher a little visit after graduation, I glanced over the recipe and started gathering my materials. Fire Drake's liver, mandrake root, Duxion's…

"Megumin, what are you going to make with *those* ingredients? Hey, what happened to your healing potion? Ink's looking pretty low; we should give her something…" Yunyun had looked over anxiously in my direction, observing me putting something together.

"This is a secret between a *friend* and me, so I can hardly tell you, my rival, what I am doing."

"Hey! Wh-whatever! What, are you getting me back for not telling you what I talked to Funifura and Dodonko about?!"

I ignored Yunyun, throwing the very expensive collection of ingredients into a mortar.

"Fine, I'll help Ink myself…!"

Finally, I glanced over at Yunyun. Ink, still looking limp and tired, was on her desk, and Yunyun was struggling to make a healing potion.

"Our household follows a high-impact educational model, so please do not baby our pet too much."

"Putting her in your bag and swinging her around isn't high impact! It's cruel! She's just a kitten! You should be more careful with her!"

Yunyun was acting awfully short-tempered as she patted Ink.

Despite her protests, I had a feeling this cat could not be done in so easily. She climbed all over people and was all-around brazen, not to mention that as she was a kitten, she could and would eat anything. But there was something rather un-catlike about her. Maybe she was just adapting to the unforgiving conditions of my house?

"Well, whatever. Let us make potions! Observe my magical skill! I shall strike down illness with a single blow! Bwa-ha-ha-ha-ha-ha...!"

"Whatever you're making over there, it's not a poison, is it? You're making something that's *good* for people, aren't you?! I heard something about striking things down in a single blow!" Yunyun frowned in distress as I began the process of crafting my very difficult potion—

First, powder the dried Fire Drake's liver. Then, take the mandrake root (full of vitality) and...

"Eek! There are specks of *fire* coming from Megumin's bowl! Megumin, what the heck are you making?!"

"Yikes! The fire's coming over to me! Argh, it's spreading! Teacher, Teacherrrr!"

"*Create Water!*" someone shouted—a shout I ignored as I grabbed a cleaver to chop up my mandrake root...

"Hey! Some of the mandrakes are running away! Who's even using mandrakes?"

"...?! Uh, that plant that's catching your cleaver in its hands, Megumin... That's a mandrake, isn't it...?"

I heard the question, but I was busy subduing the surprisingly resilient mandrake; eventually I managed to chop it up and put it in my pot… But there was still more to do. I had to catch the mandrakes that had escaped…

"Hello. I think I've got something of yours. I don't know what you're making over here, but it sure looks interesting." Arue had one of the mandrakes by the leaves; she flipped up her eye patch with one finger and handed the plant to me, grinning.

"I am making a very difficult sickness-curing potion. Have you finished with your own potion, Arue? If you're not busy, I would appreciate some help."

"Fine by me. Let's see, we can start by chopping this guy up…"

"Excellent, Arue, hold him down so he can't resist! He is a plant monster; you need not feel bad for him! Grrr, stop resisting! You want me to get out the vegetable grater?"

Arue helped me with the potion; Yunyun, meanwhile, watched us struggle at our work, her face pale. "Aww… Ahhh-ah-ah…" Her face was streaked with tears. I could feel her watching me as I safely finished off the mandrake and went for my final ingredient.

The Duxion is a duck-like monster, rare and quite cute, that always carries with it the onion that serves as its main source of food. And I needed it…!

"I won't let you do it! I won't let you go any further!" Yunyun exclaimed suddenly, grabbing my hand.

"What are you doing? Please don't interfere with my potion making."

"But! But! D-D-Duxions are just so cute…!" She shook her head, tears flying.

Somewhere along the line, the other students had started to look like they were going to break into tears, too, and I had become the center of attention. As had the Duxion, which looked at me curiously with its moist eyes.

It was cute, I had to admit. But even so…

"Yunyun, as cute as it is, it's a monster, remember? The world is full of monsters that look harmless but are in fact deadly. Why, we have

the Leisure Girl right here near our very village, don't we? A monster that evokes a powerful protective instinct in its victims so that they can never leave its side and are forced to dote upon it until the end of their days. However sweet a monster may appear, one must not hesitate to destroy it."

"I know that! I do, but—!!" Yunyun still wasn't giving in.

Arue plopped a hand on her shoulder. "C'mon—calm down. Just what part of the Duxion do you need for your potion, Megumin? If it's an internal organ, we'll have to wring its neck, but otherwise…"

Yunyun looked at me tremblingly.

"The ingredient I need is the onion it's carrying," I said. "Does that make you feel better?" I flashed her a reassuring smile.

Apparently, it did, because Yunyun gave a sigh of relief and let go of my hand.

"Onions have long been said to possess curative properties," Arue explained. "Prescriptions include eating onions, wrapping the site in onions, and, in some cases, jabbing the onion right up the problem area. The Duxion's onion is supposed to be the highest-quality onion you can find." As she spoke, she relieved the Duxion of several sprigs of its onion and started cutting them up.

As for me, I looked at Yunyun. "My word… Just what do you take me for? Even I have at least the basic decency to care for an adorable living creature. I don't seek to take life unnecessarily."

"O-of course not. I'm sorry! Phew… It's just that I've heard Duxions are worth a ton of experience points, and they're supposed to be absolutely delicious, too, so I thought…"

"………"

A rare monster worth tons of experience points?

Absolutely delicious?

"I'm really sorry. I was thinking, you know, that it would have been three birds with one stone for you—your ingredients, experience points, and lunch, so…"

"Kyu!"

The Duxion gave a little yelp and went limp when I strangled it.

I looked at my Adventurer's Card: I had gained two levels at a stroke, meaning two additional skill points to spend.

I proudly showed the card to Yunyun, whose mouth was working open and shut silently.

"Look who got some new levels."

"How could yoooooooooou?!"

6

After class.

"What do you want, Duxion Slayer? Why are we here?"

"Megumin, you'd better apologize to Yunyun, okay? I think she really took this morning hard. She's been moping around ever since."

Funifura and Dodonko had only just opened their mouths. We were back behind the school building, where I had called them.

"The next time you call me Duxion Slayer, you will be in for it. In any case, the events of this morning—which traumatized not just Yunyun but a great many of our classmates—were ultimately inspired by the two of you. Do you know what I was making?"

Funifura and Dodonko looked at each other.

"You can't be saying…"

"That potion you're holding…"

"Precisely: This is my own sickness-curing potion."

Both of them looked profoundly disturbed.

"I sympathize. I know you must be worried. However, I followed the recipe exactly, so there won't be any problems. All right, I may have gone a bit heavy on the ingredients, but I assume that will only make it *more* effective. Come on, now—take it."

"Uh…" Funifura, still obviously concerned, slowly reached out and reluctantly took the bottle.

"There," I said. "Now you no longer need the money you borrowed from Yunyun. You shall return that money to me in exchange for that potion."

"What? J-just a second—we don't even know if it's going to work…!"

I didn't let Funifura go any further. "That hardly matters. Nor does the question of whether your little brother is even actually ill, Funifura."

My intent was to shut them up.

"Ergh… L-look, that's…"

"I-it's totally true! Funifura's kid brother is totally sick!" Dodonko interjected.

But, as I had said, I didn't care. "What I'm trying to say is, you took advantage of a lonely young woman's good heart to weasel money out of her. That girl happens to be the second smartest person in class after me. She's not stupid, understand? I promise you she noticed how suspicious I thought this whole thing was, and still she—"

I stalked closer to them as I spoke; they backed up, blanching.

"Look, okay?! We'll give back the stupid money! Geez, your eyes—they're, like, completely red!"

"Don't get so angry! Y-you're scaring me!"

Then they coughed up the money Yunyun had given them.

Oops, looks like I got dangerously serious for a moment there.

When a member of the Crimson Magic Clan gets very emotional, the red glow of their eyes increases. At this rate, I was at risk of sacrificing my cool image.

"…Very well. I shall return this money to Yunyun. If you truly approached her in a spirit of friendship, that's one thing, but if you were just looking to get something out of her, then please stop. Otherwise, when I have finally learned my magic, the first thing I'll test it on will be you two."

"G-geez, we get it! 'Very well,' she says. Her eyes are still bright red! You're, like, totally in love with Yunyun!"

"We won't get between you two anymore, so just go have fun…!"

Funifura and Dodonko kept saying……… What?

"…I believe you are misinformed. I am not particularly close to Yunyun… For that matter, we are not even friends."

"Yeah, sure, just leave us alone."

"You did all this for her, and then you say you're not even friends? What are you, then?"

The two of them fanned their cheeks in annoyance as if to say, *Ooh, it's steamy.*

"What do you mean, what are we? We're just, you know…rivals, I suppose…"

"Uh-huh, yeah, sure. Seriously, whatever you say. All I can tell you is that from where we're standing, it looks awfully lovey-dovey between you two."

"Megumin, your eyes say it all… The problem for us Crimson Magic Clan members is that we can't lie when we're like that."

…………

"Anyway, we give up this time. But don't let being head of the class go to your head."

"Yeah, she's right. While the two of you are busy making eyes at each other, the rest of us might come from behind and pass you right by. If *I* become the best student in class, your precious wife might just think I'm her new rival, eh? You'd better watch out so we don't—"

I didn't care to let them finish their parting shots; I simply attacked.

"Hey! Argh, you just gave me this potion—don't break it! No fair, you're the worst! S-stoooop…!"

"L-learn to read a crowd! You *have* to have a parting shot when…! Hey, don't…!"

7

My counterattack on the girls complete, I went back to the classroom with a light heart and a smile on my face to get Ink and my bag. When I stepped inside, I found Yunyun in there by herself, looking despondent. "...What are you doing here all alone?"

"What do you mean, what am I doing here?! I was waiting for you, Megumin! You just left Ink and ran off somewhere!"

I guess she had been waiting to go home with me.

"Oh, I just had some business with Funifura," I replied.

As I realized that Yunyun and I now, apparently, had made a routine of walking home together, Funifura's and Dodonko's words echoed in my mind.

...W-well, in light of the recent sightings of the Dark God's servant, we could afford to set aside our rivalry for the time being. No, I would not call us friends, but in troubled times like these...

Sure, Yunyun sounded angry, but the relief on her face after she had been sitting there by herself was far more evident.

"You had something to do with Funifura? That's unusual. Anyway, let's go home. We should hurry—Teacher said they're resealing the god tonight..."

"Here, this is for you." As Yunyun got ready to go, I gave her the money from Funifura.

Yunyun stood there with the little pouch of coins in her hand, looking completely flummoxed. I grabbed my bag as if to say we were done here. I tried to stuff Ink inside, but for some reason she just wouldn't go. She dug her claws into my shoulder and resisted mightily.

"Megumin, this money..."

"It is from Funifura. I guess she managed to get medicine for her brother somehow. So she wanted to give that back to you. Isn't that nice?"

I continued trying to peel Ink off my shoulder.

D-dumb cat! Did she really hate being in my bag that much?

Just as our battle was really heating up, Yunyun said, "Say, uh. Did you...do anything for Funifura's brother? I mean, you... You were working on a sickness-curing potion or something..." She was practically mumbling by this point.

Behold, Funifura, Dodonko. I told you she was the second smartest student after me.

"Would a pragmatist like me do something so unlikely to yield any personal benefit?"

"Well, that's…actually an extremely persuasive way of looking at it."

………

"Hey, why are you leaving all of a sudden?! I've been waiting ages for you! Don't ditch me!"

Outside, the sun was sinking in the west, and soon it would be evening.

Yunyun rushed to catch up with me. Ink, who completely refused to go in my bag, was perched on my shoulder as I walked along the road home.

"Megumin, you really *didn't* do anything, did you?"

"You are a skeptical one. Say I had made some kind of medicine for Funifura's little brother. It would be no trouble to anyone, so what's the harm?"

"I—I think you harmed a lot of girls in potions class this morning…"

I didn't respond, just kept walking silently along. Yunyun picked up her pace so she could walk alongside me. She glanced over and said, "…Listen, Megumin. I'm not, you know, saying thank you or anything, but… You want to stop somewhere on the way home? I've got my money back and all. I'll treat you to something."

This time it was my turn to glance at her. She was smiling.

…It looked like my rival had already figured out more or less what had happened. She was just that smart.

8

"I did say I'd treat you. I'll admit that. But, um…"

We had left the shop and were on the way home again. Yunyun was peering into her wallet and sighing.

"And a fine treat it was. This is the first time since the day I was born that I've had so much to eat. I don't think I could take another bite the rest of the day."

"Well, thank goodness for that! Oh, *sigh*… I know I said you could eat as much as you wanted, but…!" Yunyun's miffed voice sounded along the twilit road.

"Phew… It is indeed difficult to walk after eating so much. Maybe we should take a rest somewhere until I've digested a bit?"

"Argh… Just, argh…! How much of a glutton do you have to be to eat that much anyway…?!" Yunyun sounded partly angry and partly just exasperated.

In due course, we came upon the village's park. Well, *park* might be a strong word: It was just a bench, a pond, and a small structure in case it rained. I peeled Ink off my shoulder and lay on my back on the bench.

"M-Megumin! Your skirt! Anyone can walk by and see your underwear! Oh, for…! That's not very ladylike…"

Yunyun gallantly flipped my skirt back down for me.

"I think you will make an excellent wife, Yunyun. Perhaps you could take care of me after we graduate? I promise you, I am the kind of person who will eat your food every day and still be sure to say it's delicious."

"N-no way! Why should I?! You think calling my food delicious is all it takes?! Just…telling me my cooking is delicious every day… Every day… Hmmmm…"

Suddenly she seemed on the fence about it. Naive as always.

Maybe it was these absurd exchanges that made Funifura and Dodonko claim we were all lovey-dovey.

"Speaking of graduation, what do you plan to do after I'm gone, Yunyun? I'll be able to graduate with just one more skill-up potion, you know."

"What? How'd that happen? I was sure you told me you needed another four points to reach your magic. So after yesterday's skill-up potion, you should be at three to go, just like me...... Oh!!" Then it struck her. "The Duxion this morning! You strangled that Duxion, and your level—!"

"Went up by two, yes. A total of three skill points when combined with yesterday's potion. I need only one more before I have enough points to learn my spell. I assume I will graduate after the next test."

Ink climbed onto my tummy. How could she be so brazen?

Yunyun's voice was small; she sounded on the verge of tears as she said, "I—I can't believe it... We won't be able to graduate together...? After I worked so hard to match our skill points..."

She sniffled a little...

...and I sat up ramrod straight, sending Ink tumbling off me.

"What did you just say?" I demanded. "Have you specifically been manipulating your skill points so you could graduate alongside me? Was your failure to get into the top three on yesterday's test deliberate, so as not to earn yourself a skill-up potion?"

"?!" Yunyun flinched, an *oops* look on her face. That was all the confirmation I needed.

"What kind of a fool?! If you were that eager to graduate together, then just put off learning your spell until we're both ready, no matter how many skill points you have! For that matter, you couldn't just hold off learning Advanced Magic or tell me you wanted to graduate together; you had to resort to this? There's foolish and then there's downright stupid!"

"B-b-but, but, Megumin, you were always so far ahead of me, and then all of a sudden I was past you! I was so sure you were going to graduate first...!"

"Ah! You just said you got past me! You have not! You have by no means passed me! In this very special case, I will tell you the truth: I have no interest in learning Advanced Magic! I have my eye on a killer spell far more powerful than that! Behold my Adventurer's Card! I long ago earned enough points for mere Advanced Magic!"

I jumped up from the bench in my fervor, holding my card under Yunyun's nose. She studied it intently.

"Y-you really do…! Phew, I knew you were more amazing than me, Megumin…!"

"What? …Uh, yes. Well, I am amazing. Thus, *ahem*, it would be most problematic for me were you to hold back."

It was awkward enough just to have Yunyun standing there grinning, obviously thrilled about this. Maybe she really did just want the strongest possible rival.

"Y-yeah. I'm sorry about that. But a spell more incredible than anything in advanced magic? What, do you want to learn blasting magic? Or…don't tell me…detonation magic…?"

"I speak of Explosion."

…………That shut Yunyun up for a while.

"Um, did I…hear you right? It sounded like you said 'Explosion.'"

"Yes, Explosion. A spell most incredible, often called the strongest of magics."

Yunyun went quiet again, until…

"What are you talking about? You mean Explosion, like, *that* Explosion? The one everyone calls a gimmick? The spell that demands more skill points than anything else anyone of any class will ever learn, and that even if you do learn it, you probably can't use it, and that even if you can use it, one burst will leave you paralyzed because you have no MP left?"

"Yes. That is the Explosion I'm talking about." I nodded.

Yunyun took a deep breath and…!

"What are you, stupid?! Megumin, what are you even talking about?! What could you possibly do with that spell?! Most people who learn it don't even have the MP to use it, remember? And if you some-how managed, the best you could hope for would be once a day. It's a gimmick with no practical applications, okay?! What are you thinking?! Have you gone nuts?! They say genius and idiocy are just a stone's throw apart from each other! Megumin, have you crossed that line?!"

"Yunyun, I will not abide any more of this talk of stupidness and idiocy, even from you! ...Anyway, I am well aware of the details by now. I have done more research on Explosion than anyone else. I daresay I am the most knowledgeable person in this village today when it comes to Explosion."

"If you know so much about it, then why do you want to learn it?! Megumin, you... If you learn Advanced Magic like you're supposed to... If you start gaining some experience... You could be the sort of wizard whose name goes down in history...! So why?!"

For some reason, my choice moved Yunyun to tears.

We had come this far. I gave her the honest answer. "It is, of course, because I love Explosion."

Yunyun's eyes were wide; maybe she had been expecting some deeper reason. "...I take it back, Megumin. You're not a genius; you *are* an idiot."

"I warned you you would pay for any more idiot talk!"

I launched myself at Yunyun!

9

"*Huff... Puff...!* I won...! For the first time in my life, I beat you, Megumin...!" Yunyun's face was shining, and she was clearly happy from the bottom of her heart.

Un... Unbelievable...!

For the first time in my life, I had lost to Yunyun.

"*Ahem*, well, it's true I was not giving this battle my full attention.

You know how it is. I am the sort of person whose power wanes with the moon."

"I know that's not true. You're not a demon or something! Just admit you lost!"

Yunyun had me pinned after our tussle in the otherwise empty park. The cool earth felt good against my flushed skin.

The sun was going down. Both of us were breathing hard.

The blood had gone to my head, and I let myself get involved in hand-to-hand combat, not a specialty of mine.

"*Sigh...* I admit it—I lost, so please let me go. I lost, okay? Uncle."

Yunyun politely let me go.

"...Phew, yes, I lost. I suppose it's only to be expected, me having eaten so much. If I had to quantify it, I would say I wasn't able to use half my usual strength."

"Hey! You can't start making up excuses now that I've let you go!"

Yunyun was obviously distressed, but I simply stood up, brushing the dirt off my knees. "I'm glad you were able to win once before I left on my journey. You'll be the chief of this place one day, Yunyun. While I am out making my name as a wizard of great renown in the world, you can grow old leading a perfectly ordinary life here in the village."

"Couldn't you just stop at 'I'm glad you won'?! You just have to twist the knife. You actually *do* feel bad about losing, don't you?! ... Hey, wait... You're going on some kind of journey when you graduate?" Yunyun asked nervously.

I picked up Ink, who had inched closer to my feet. "Yes indeed I am. I will tell you and you alone, Yunyun. But there is in fact a reason for my love of Explosion."

Ink had affixed herself to the shoulder of my robe once again; it seemed to be her favorite spot. I gave her a nice scratch on the head as I revealed to Yunyun something I had never even told my parents.

"When I was young, I was once attacked by a magical beast. A wizard woman who happened to be passing by dispatched the creature with Explosion. The destructive force of that blast. The overwhelming violence. The absolute power. It was staggering, truly fit to be called the most powerful of spells. Seeing it just that one time was enough to rob me of any desire to learn anything else."

The hooded woman's voice and presence were hazy in my memory now, but the explosion—that remained etched in my mind's eye as clearly as the day I saw it. Just remembering it was enough to make my chest hot and tight.

I had no interest in the romantic gossip Funifura and Dodonko liked to share, nor did I have any noble goals like Yunyun, working so hard to become the leader of our clan. All I wanted in life was to see that hooded woman one more time and to show her my own explosion.

I wanted to see her and say thank you.

Then I would ask her: *What did you think of my explosion? Of the magic I learned from you?*

When I had finished telling Yunyun about this, my one and only dream, all the disapproval disappeared from her face. She looked almost relieved, nearly as if she understood.

"With a story like that, how can I object? An explosion wizard really walks a path of thorns, though. With your MP, Megumin, I think you can probably use the spell, but then you won't be able to move. A journey is all well and good, but if you do it alone, then what if you use your magic, can't move, and some other monster finds you defenseless on the ground and attacks you? Do you have anyone who can go with you?"

"I have about as many friends as you do, so of course I don't."

"Why do you sound proud of that?! Hey, you won't leave on your journey, you know, the minute you learn your magic, right? You'll stay in the village for a while, right?"

"Well, I suppose. I can hardly leave my little sister to her own devices, so most likely I will find part-time work in the village and wait for the right opportunity to leave." That seemed to give Yunyun some peace of mind. "As for you, Yunyun, you will stay in this village permanently to become the new chief, won't you? The position is hereditary, after all."

"Yeah. I guess I'll be chief someday. But before that, I want to have other experiences. Right now, I still need you to rescue me and stuff, Megumin, but someday…"

Just when it looked like Yunyun was about to say something important, there was a small sound and Ink twitched. It was a splashing of water. We looked over and—

"Oh, you don't see one of those every day! A wild Duxion! Right here in the middle of the village…"

The Duxion had been swimming in the pond; now it came toward us, obviously feeling quite safe. Despite how delicious and experience-rich they were, Duxions had some unique trait that kept other monsters from attacking them. One scholar had theorized that Duxions were so cute, even other monsters felt protective of them.

The Duxion came out of the pond and waddled toward us, its big, moist eyes on Yunyun. She crouched down so as not to scare the creature. With a gentle smile on her face, she finished what she had been saying earlier.

"…Right now, I still need your help, Megumin. But someday, I'm going to be the number one wizard in the village and protect the weak and helpless, like this Duxion, who…"

"Kyu!"

I didn't really hear what she was saying, though, because I was more interested in making sure the Duxion didn't get away before I wrung its neck.

I held up the limp monster triumphantly. "Score one dinner for Megumin!"

"How could yoooooooooooou?!" Yunyun cried, flinging herself at me.

Round two!

10

"...Sheesh. It's your fault, Yunyun, that it is practically fully dark now."

"My fault?! How is it my fault?! For that matter, how can you bring yourself to strangle such a sweet living thing? You're always so ruthless, Megumin! You could stand to have a conscience, you know!"

Yunyun went ahead of me, still angry.

Thanks to our little rematch, it was now quite dark outside. Magical streetlamps illuminated the roads around the village.

"We each have one win and one loss. In other words, a draw. I believe we can agree that is the same as saying there were no contests today."

"N-no, we can't! I beat you, and that's a fact! I finally got a victory, and nothing can change that! They don't cancel each other out. It's one win and one loss for each of us, and don't you forget it! Heh-heh, I'll have to be sure to write about today in my diary. I'll write, 'Today, I beat Megumin'!"

"Be certain to include that after that, you were shoved helplessly to the ground and rendered powerless."

"I don't recognize that! You need to stop using Ink as a shield! ...I wonder why she likes you so much, considering how you treat her." Yunyun looked at Ink, puzzled, but the black cat just held on to my shoulder and yawned.

She truly was a strange animal. Normally, all that flailing about would cause a cat to run away or at least start meowing.

I took the spoils of my victory—the Duxion—and hurried home. Yunyun had treated me to a meal, but I was sure my little sister was going hungry. I wanted to get back so she could eat my trophy.

Yunyun glanced at me as I walked along, holding the Duxion and humming a little tune. "Megumin, are you sure you're a girl? Where's your coyness? Flirtatiousness?"

"What about you, Yunyun? Are you sure you're the chief's daughter?

Did you leave your Crimson Magic Clan member's sense of theatricality someplace?"

We stopped and stood for a moment, silent, then sidled up to each other, improbable smiles on our faces.

One win, one loss today.

I was hoping to settle things right here, but Yunyun glanced away. "*Sigh*... Why are you like this, Megumin, day after day?"

"I would like to ask you the same thing. Why do you come after me every day?" I grinned.

"Erk... W-well..." Yunyun tried to throw me off by starting to walk again. I followed behind her, still smirking. "...Gosh! And just when I thought today might end up a good day, finally! Are you not happy until you've pulled something on me every single day, Megumin? Whatever party you join in the future, I swear you'll be nothing but trouble for them!"

"I do not know what you're talking about. The day I learn explosion magic, I will be a source of the greatest firepower for any party, able to blow away even a general of the Demon King. And any party I, the greatest genius of the Crimson Magic clan, might join would have to be an elite assembly composed entirely of advanced classes...!"

I faced Yunyun, picturing the future party I had not yet met, when suddenly a loud, high-pitched sound echoed through the streets of the village. It was the bell they rang when there was an emergency. Wondering what could be going on, we turned toward the sound...

We were greeted by the sight of a numberless swarm of monsters flying up into the night sky. They spread out in every direction, almost as if they were looking for something...!

"M... M-M-Megumin! Those things! Th-th-those are...!"

"C-c-c-calm down, Yunyun. Didn't the teacher say that the resealing of the Dark God was going to be '*forcible*' or something?! And I believe our careless instructor also talked about having something special ready in case they failed! So I'm sure this problem will be solved shortly!"

Heck, our teacher had practically *wanted* to fail, as far as I could tell. Hence, I assumed there was nothing to worry about. It even occurred to me that perhaps our teacher had deliberately let things go wrong.

Ink had scurried down from my shoulder and, surprisingly, into the bag she hated so much. I guess even the bold kitten was intimidated by a swarm of monsters.

"Hey... H-hey!" Yunyun shouted, tugging at my sleeve as I buried Ink in the bag. She was looking at the sky and her face was pale. "Are they coming this way?"

She pointed up, up at the monsters who were, indeed, clearly making their way toward us.

"We have to run! My house is closest to here! Yunyun, no matter what happens to me, you must keep fighting! Don't look back! I will let you handle things here while I go on ahead!"

When Yunyun heard that...!

"Y-you idiot! What are you talking about?! Megumin, I could never leave you behi— Wait, what? What did you say?! Tell me what you said!"

Yunyun had not been kind enough to miss my final words and protested tearfully. I glanced back—ignoring her—and found the monsters cruising easily through the sky toward us.

"Y-Yunyun, how many skill points do you have?! Do you not yet have enough to learn Advanced Magic at this very moment?!"

"Of course not! But, Megumin, if you forget about Explosion and take Advanced Magic right now, you could clean up those monsters with one spell! Come on, do it, pleeease!"

Yunyun appealed to me, again tearfully, but on this point, I could not budge! Learning explosion magic had been the focus of everything I had done in my life!

"There is no hope; they're right on top of— Huh?"

"...They went right past us."

Several of the monsters had indeed swooped over our heads without so much as noticing us, flying off somewhere else.

I let out a breath of relief and looked in the direction where the bell was still ringing. I saw several bright bursts of light illuminating the night sky. I was certain they marked where the village adults were exercising their powers. I was confident they would soon have the situation under control. But we still needed to get home quickly.

"Yunyun, you should come home with me. Stay at my house tonight."

"What? S-stay at—? Can I?!"

"But of course. What with all the monsters wandering around, I can't imagine you want to go all the way to your own house. I will lend you some of my pajamas, but if you complain that the chest is too tight or the pants are too short, I will make you sleep naked."

"I—I won't complain! I can live with that, believe me!"

She did not, however, deny that the chest might be a little tight or the pants a little short.

I contemplated starting round three, but we didn't have time for it with things the way they were.

"We are almost to my house. Let's go quickly. My little sister is the only one at home today. She will be starving by now, but I'm sure she will have locked the doors and will be looking after the house. It is a cramped, ramshackle place, but as long as the doors are locked, even those monsters can't—"

—*get inside.*

I didn't finish my sentence.

The Duxion in my hand dropped to the ground.

I stared uncomprehendingly at the smashed door of our house and whispered:

".........Komekko?"

A Chicken-and-Egg Bowl for This Village Girl

"All right, Lady Komekko. Here I thought we had this puzzle all figured out, but look what we've got next."

"I don't know what it says. You read it, Great Lord Host."

………

"Listen, let's stop with the Great-Lord-Host business. You just call me Host, and I'll just call you Komekko."

"Okay."

We nodded at each other, and then Host read the words that had shown up on the tomb.

"*'O you who would break the seal, make thee an offering upon the altar. The sacrifice is to be a hen and its offspring. Offer them here together with your prayers…'* I can't quite read the end of it, but I guess it's, like, you know, a living sacrifice or whatever. A chicken and its kid, huh? Sacrifices are always best when they're the richest, showiest stuff you can find. It won't be easy to find these in the forest…"

Host was muttering about something. He sounded worried, but then he clapped his hands.

"All right! I've got it, Komekko. I'll give you some money, so you hit the village and buy me a hen and its chick! The best you can find!"

"All right!"

I grabbed the money he offered me and set off for the village.

An hour later…

"I'm back! I got the stuff!"

"Aww, way to go, that's… Hey, what the heck is that?" When Host saw what I was carrying, balancing it on a tray so it wouldn't fall, he seemed surprised.

I set the tray carefully on the altar.

"Living Sacrifice Chicken-and-Egg Bowl."

"You blockhead!"

Host opened the lid of the dish I'd brought and looked inside…

"Ahhh. Lookit you. You're right—that's definitely a chicken and its kid in there, but I'll be damned if there's a seal in the world that'll open for a chicken-and-egg bowl. Dang, and here I thought I was finally going to meet Lady Wolbach's other half…"

"What kind of person is Lady Wolbach?"

"Hmm? Her true form, it's, like, this huuuuge black beast. I swear, it'd have you shaking in your boots… Grrr, I guess this is one job I've got to do myself. Fine, it'll take a while, but…"

Then he spread his wings to fly somewhere. Just before he lifted off, though, Host glanced at me.

"…So listen. That means I won't be around for a while, but I will see you again. We can play together when I get back—just don't tell anyone about me, okay? …You can go ahead and eat the chicken-and-egg bowl."

Then he launched himself into the air.

I didn't know how long it had been. I was sitting in front of the altar, finishing the last of the food.

"?"

Suddenly I heard a rustling from the bushes. When I looked over, I saw an inky-black magical beast crawling toward me.

…It was really small, though.

I kept eating my chicken-and-egg bowl quickly in surprise as the beast made its way over to me. It looked like it was after my food. Almost like it thought this chicken-and-egg bowl belonged to it…but Host had given it to *me*.

I stood up, still eating, and the enraged beast attacked me!

I suffered a few scratches here and there, but after a long and grueling clash, the magical beast finally sat still, as if it had given up.

Specifically, it had resigned itself to its place in my arms, where I was gnawing on its head.

I woooon!

I took my hard-earned prize and went home.

Chapter
5

Prelude to
Explosion
Madness

1

It sounded like the inside of my tiny tumbledown house was being torn apart.

Someone was in the building, and they were looking for something.

Who was the someone? One of those monsters. It had to be.

And inside the house with it was—

"K-K… Komekko… My Komekko…"

"M-Megumin, calm down! J-j-just calm down, okay?!" Yunyun grabbed me by the shoulders and shook me as I unsteadily faced the ruined entryway.

"My Komekkooooooooooo!"

"Stop that! I told you, we have to stay calm!!"

Her words brought me back to reality, and my brain went into overdrive.

She was right: At a time like this, the key was to keep cool and think.

"It's all right! My little sister is in fact the reincarnation of Astroborg, the deity of violent hunger! In a crisis, her seal will be broken, and she and I will at last conquer the world!"

"Calm down! Stay with me!"

"Hrgf?!" Yunyun grabbed my cheeks and pulled, bringing me back to reality once again. "Eeeyow-ow... This is no time to be talking such foolishness, Yunyun! My sister must be in the house. We have to rush in and save her! A girl as street smart and brave as she is would never become monster food so easily! Come on—there's no time to waste!"

"...Wh-why do I have a bad feeling about this...?" Yunyun grumbled, but she followed me just the same, taking out the dagger at her hip, its silver blade gleaming.

"For once your eccentricities serve me well, Yunyun. I do not have any weapon worthy of the name. If the need arises, I will be counting on you, all right?"

"Eccentricities?! What eccentricities?! Hey, did I do something weird again?!"

"Weird? Let's just say that you are the only girl I know who would bring her favorite bladed weapon to school."

"Urgh... W-well, you're right about that, but...still! Seriously, what is this unsettling feeling I keep having...?"

I hushed the querulous Yunyun with a finger to my lips, and then we sneaked into the rattling house.

I heard nothing resembling Komekko screaming. For an instant, my mind imagined the worst possible things, but I kept telling myself my little sister was immune to anything really awful...!

We went in the front door...and came face-to-face with the monster.

The creature and I stared at each other: There was a birdlike beak on its reptilian face...

".........Ah, ahhhhhhhh! Yunyun, Yunyun! Yunyunyun! Yunyun!"

"Wait don't push me hold on don't screw up my name wait just wait would you?!"

"Shhhaaaaaaaaaa!"

"It's threatening us it's very threatening, Yunyun, gut it with your dagger!"

"But, but I can't suddenly— How, I can't kill a monster…!"

The monster howled menacingly at us, the two yammering girls in front of it. Yunyun held her knife out, but she was shaking a little and looked like she might burst into tears at any moment. The monster observed her, then, probably deciding we were easy pickings, spread its arms wide and moved in…

"Now's your chance!" I exclaimed. Yunyun stabbed the monster in the belly using the momentum of me shoving her from behind. The creature screamed.

"Hiiigyaaaaaaa!"

"Eeeeeeeeeeek!"

Yunyun, the unfortunate stabber of the monster, also screamed.

The monster rolled around in the entryway. I grabbed the knife from Yunyun—who was still screaming—clutched it in both hands, and drove it into the creature's neck.

"Wa— Waaaaaaaaah! Megumin! M-Megumin, you—!"

"P-pipe down already, Yunyun! We are Crimson Magic Clan members, whom even the Demon King fears; can we hesitate to exterminate a mere…monster…?"

………?

The monster I had stabbed looked…*off* somehow. Wait…

"…It disappeared?"

"But…why?"

After a few moments of suffering from its neck wound, the creature had turned to black smoke and vanished. What did it mean that it had left no corpse behind?

Then I realized that the noise in the house had stopped. That seemed to suggest the monster we had just killed had been the only one searching in here. Yet, I had been sure we saw quite a number of monsters heading in the direction of our house.

What had it even been doing here, ransacking a shack of a place that hardly had so much as food on the shelves?

No, there were more important things to worry about now!

"...That's right: Komekko! Komekko, where are you?! It's me! Your big sister is here!"

"K-Komekko? Komekko!"

Yunyun and I tore through the house, but Komekko didn't respond to any of our calls. A thorough investigation of the place revealed no traces of blood.

That might have meant she had already gotten away. Or been carried off by those monsters...

"Yunyun, outside! I'm sure my little sister must be outside. I will go look for her. You stay here in case she comes home before I do. Shove the furniture up against the front door as a barricade. Oh, and I'm going to need to borrow this dagger for a bit."

I excused myself and made to leave when I felt Yunyun grab my collar.

"N-no, you can't! Megumin, you can hardly survive gym class! You'll get eaten alive out there! I'm going with you!"

Grrr...

"That little taste of victory over me earlier certainly has given you a smart mouth. But very well, let us go together, then. That being the case, Yunyun, I will let you handle any monsters that appear."

"What?! I-I'm not sure I...can..."

As we spoke, Yunyun and I drifted outside...

...and came face-to-face with a monster tearing apart the bag I had left out there.

"Ink! Didn't you put Ink in that bag?!"

Yunyun's shout caused this next monster to notice us.

"Th-there's no hope for her now; we have to leave her behind! We can memorialize her with a proper grave later to honor her valiant sacrifice on our behalf! It's all right—she will still be with us. Yes, she will always be in our hearts…"

"She's alive! Will you *look* already? She's right there! It's too soon to give up!"

Yunyun grabbed the nape of my neck as I tried to flee from the monster. She pointed at my bag. I could indeed see Ink crawling out from among its tattered remains. The monster, though, seemed to mean no harm; it simply watched her go. For that matter, it showed no interest in us, either.

"I don't know what's going on, but this is our chance! That fuzz ball seems to have provoked the creature's maternal instincts or some such! Now is our moment to get out of here and find my sister…!"

"Wait! Please, please help Ink, too! I know how worried you are about Komekko, but please!"

"What are you saying? If we steal Ink from a monster that is clearly deeply attached to her, I am sure it will attack us! Mostly sure anyway!"

Yunyun looked at me like a child begging her parents to keep a puppy they had found.

…*Argh, how irritating!*

"You get ready to run!" I said. "I am going to get back the fuzz ball my sister has been raising so diligently!"

Raising as emergency provisions, to be more specific—but I left out that part.

Yunyun's face lit up, while I took the dagger and sneaked around behind the beast…

…and found the monster follow suit and move at the same time.

The creature reached out and took Ink in both its clawed hands. She didn't resist its embrace but was, in fact, quite calm. The monster spread its wings and prepared to leap into the sky…!

"If I let them take that cat, my little sister, who has been waiting so patiently for her to grow up, will never forgive me! Behold my knife-throwing technique!"

"Ahhh!" Yunyun cried.

I flung the dagger, and it sailed off into the distance.

"...Dastardly! Who knew it would protect itself with a wind barrier...?!"

"It didn't protect itself with anything! You obviously just can't throw straight to save your life!"

"This is no time for an argument over a minor detail! Ink is—!"

"I know! You're right, Megumin, but this whole situation has just felt really wrong to me from the first minute!"

While Yunyun and I quarreled, the monster carrying Ink swept up into the sky and started flying away...

As we watched Ink being carried off, I mused in a strikingly calm voice, "...I am certain that cat was an angel from heaven. She is simply going back to her home. Hence, we mustn't cry but watch her depart with gladness..."

"Don't just give up on Ink because of some weird scenario you just created in your head! What are we going to do? She's been kidnapped! What do we do; what do we do?!" Yunyun collected the dagger but was nearly in tears.

"Well, now, calm down. Considering Ink did not fight back when the monster picked her up, I don't think she's in much danger. Life in my house has trained her well to detect imminent bodily harm."

"Hey, how exactly have you been raising that cat?! You haven't been torturing her, have you?!" Yunyun grabbed my shoulders and shook.

In any event, Komekko was more important than Ink right now.

"We must let Ink go for the time being. Komekko is what matters. My little sister is quite tough and resourceful. She is not one of those soft girls who would weep and cry and get themselves brutally killed. She must be here somewhere..."

"Y-you're right! Do you have any idea where Komekko would be likely to go, Megumin?!"

Someplace she would be likely to go...

I couldn't possibly guess.

But wait… Something Komekko had said recently nagged at me. What was it? What had she said…?

"It's not an idea, precisely, but call it a hunch. When I was young, I was much like Komekko…"

At least in the sense that our parents often got mad at me for leaving the house without permission.

Before I could voice this thought, a memory came back to me.

I remembered how, when I was a child, I had played with the puzzle that kept the Dark God sealed inside, considering it like a toy.

"…Oh!"

"…? What's wrong, Megumin?"

When I'd asked Komekko what she was doing outside, she had said: *"I found a toy, and I was playing with it! You wanna try it, too, Sis?"*

…Her toy.

… Could she possibly have meant…?!

"Ahhh… Ahhhh…! Sh-sh-she might be…!"

"What? Megumin, what are you muttering about all of a sudden?"

That was it! It all made sense now!

Our house was too poor to have any toys. And yet, Komekko had said she was playing with one. It was always possible that my dear little sister had wheedled a toy out of some villager, but the most likely thing was…!

2

The tomb of the Dark God loomed outside the village. Illuminated by magical lamps, the place gave off an eerie vibe, not helped by the fact that it was nighttime.

We were there despite the monsters still flying in the sky. They paid us no mind even when they did spot us, as if they were searching for something but not us.

"Hey, Megumin, whatever hunch you have, I really don't think Komekko would be—"

I didn't answer the nervous Yunyun as we spied out the situation at the tomb from our hiding place in the bushes.

".........Oh, there she is."

"...Yes indeed, she is there."

Komekko was standing in front of the tomb, her hands full of puzzle pieces, whatsoever it was she intended to do with them.

I knew they were really the pieces of the seal. Seriously, what *was* she doing with them here?

Increasingly dubious, I followed where she was looking.

"...Good news, Yunyun. It looks like our fur ball is safe."

"How can you be so calm?! This is a nightmare!"

Komekko, with the puzzle pieces in her hands, was silently facing a monster that was holding Ink.

"Ohhh, wh-wh-what do we do?! Where did the other villagers go anyway?!"

"It doesn't seem to me that any new monsters are emerging from the tomb. Once they were confident there were no more coming, I assume they scattered through the village to exterminate the rest of the beasts."

The night sky had been periodically lit up by bursts of magic from here and there around the village. If things had been different, Komekko and Yunyun and I could have been watching from the window of my house, enjoying the show like it was a fireworks display.

"In any event, remain calm. As you can see, we face only one enemy, and it is distracted by Komekko. So long as we don't let our guard down, I think we will be fine. We have already defeated one of them together."

"Y-yeah, you're right. Thanks for using your head." Seeing me logical and calm seemed to help Yunyun settle down.

Then Komekko put the puzzle pieces on the ground and threw her arms wide, approaching the monster.

"...I wonder what your sister is doing."

"Trying to intimidate it, perhaps. She appears to be attempting to make off with Ink." The monster backed away as Komekko came slowly but steadily closer. Even Ink seemed to be trembling for some reason. "It looks like she has the upper hand, and I'm rather curious to see how this will play out… But we must act now, Yunyun. Distract it, please!"

"Oka— Hey, wait! Why do I have to be the bait?!"

"Because you are too much of a wuss to kill the monster. Give me that dagger… I promise I won't throw it this time, so hand it over—quickly!"

"N-no way! I'll do it this time, I really will, so, Megumin, you go out and be the— Huh?!"

As we grappled for the knife, Yunyun happened to look up at the sky. I followed her shout and looked up to discover five additional monsters coming in for a landing around Komekko.

"W-w-we're gonna be okay, right?! Megumin, you have a plan, don't you?!"

"Of course. At desperate moments, a heretofore-dormant power always conveniently awakens or reinforcements arrive just in the nick of time. If I simply give one good girlish scream…"

"Megumin, what are you talking about?! For that matter, where are you looking?! Your eyes are so empty! Don't tell me… Do you just crumble that quickly in the face of adversity?!"

The monsters that had surrounded Komekko paid no heed to my bout of escapism but began to howl threateningly at my sister.

"Kishaaaaa!"

"Hey, Megumin! Is Komekko okay in the head?! She's getting ready to take on all those monsters by herself! She doesn't look the least bit scared, and actually, I think the monsters look more frightened of her!"

My little sister might really be quite a big deal.

Ink, I could understand. She and Komekko were natural enemies. But why were the other monsters afraid of her? It was as if Ink's fear was being communicated to them.

"Argh, we don't have time for this! ......This is the one thing I wanted to avoid, but..."

As I spoke, I pulled out my trump card—the one hanging around my neck.

Yunyun saw me. "Your Adventurer's Card? ...Huh? Megumin, you're not going to—!"

But indeed I was. Sometimes one simply has no choice. When I had to decide which was dearer to me, my little sister's life or explosion magic, the answer was clear...!

"Stop right there!"

Komekko and the monsters turned at the sound of my voice. I emerged from the bushes holding my Adventurer's Card in one hand.

"**I am Megumin. Greatest genius of the Crimson Magic Clan and wielder of advanced magic!** Now step away from my sister!"

"Oh, hey, Sis! That guy took my food!"

"Komekko?! What food are you talking about?! You don't mean Ink?!" Yunyun yelped.

I was trying to be dramatic here, but these two—!

Yunyun, dagger in hand, jumped out after me. "...Hey, Megumin, did you really learn Advanced Magic? After all that talk about how much you love Explosion?"

"...A genius of my distinction should be able to grind monsters for skill points easily enough. However long it takes, be it a few decades or more, I swear I will learn Explosion."

...In spite of my bold declaration, though, something in me still hesitated. Yes, even though I was standing face-to-face with a crowd of monsters.

During all this, the beasts had turned their attention to Yunyun and me and were moving to surround us. One of them spread its wings and bounded into the sky to attack us from the air.

The hand holding my Adventurer's Card started trembling.

This was the dream I had cherished since childhood. It wasn't easy to just throw away.

But there was no other way to protect my little sister.

...It's all right. I worked hard before, and I'll do it again.

With that thought in mind, I took my card...!

"Your voice is shaking as hard as your hand. Something's holding you back, isn't it?"

Yunyun slipped the dagger into its place on her hip as she spoke.

She had her Adventurer's Card out just like I did.

"What are you—"

—*doing?* I didn't get to ask. Instead...

"*Lightning*!!"

...I was cut off by Yunyun shouting a spell.

3

I dashed along holding Komekko by the hand, using the lamps that shined here and there to guide me.

"Sis, Yunyun was awesome, huh?! Her lightning was like, *boom*!"

Maybe it was the excitement that made Komekko grip my hand so hard.

"Yes, she was very awesome, wasn't she? But I tell you, I cannot believe that I, of all people, was beaten to the punch by Yunyun! I always thought she was so timid and hesitant!" I said regretfully and continued my search for the adults.

Yunyun had learned Intermediate Magic.

And learning magic meant you graduated from school. Graduating meant you could no longer get the rare skill-up potions that were so generously given to young members of the Crimson Magic Clan. If Yunyun wanted to learn Advanced Magic after this, she would have to do it by hunting monsters in battle to raise her level.

If I remembered right, Intermediate Magic cost ten skill points. That was how many levels she would have to gain to earn those points back. The higher one's level got, the more difficult increasing it became. Yunyun was still low-level, so she would probably gain quickly. But to gain ten levels, no matter how readily they came, would probably take at least a year.

My rival would spend the next year being treated as an inexperienced, immature member of our clan. It wouldn't matter that she had worked so hard to be worthy as the chief's daughter or that she had always had some of the best grades in class.

"Sis, are you crying?"

"I am not crying! The regret is causing my MP to come out my eyes!"

As she vaporized the head of the creature holding Ink with a lightning bolt, Yunyun told us that she would collect our cat, so I was to take Komekko, get away, and find an adult.

While I had dithered, Yunyun had ceased to be a wizard-in-training anymore. And then the girl who had always refused to harm so much as a fly had cast her spell without a moment's hesitation.

Wimp though she usually was, it seemed Yunyun could steel herself when it came to protecting someone else. Seeing my rival like that, she seemed so impossibly bright...

"...? Sis, what's wrong? Are you tired from running?"

I had stopped moving. Komekko looked up at me, puzzled.

My self-proclaimed rival was facing down those monsters alone at that moment.

My self-proclaimed rival, who had never technically defeated me even once.

My self-proclaimed rival, a strange girl with no friends who had somehow caught up with me.

If I run now for the sake of my own dreams, I will never again be able to hold my head high in combat with this girl who calls herself my rival.

"Komekko. Do you love your sister?"

"I love you!" she replied immediately, beaming.

"...Would you love her even if she couldn't use the most powerful spell? Even if she wasn't the world's most powerful older sister?"

"It's okay. Then I would become the strongest for both of us!" She was still smiling broadly.

Of course. I knew she was going to be a big deal: already seeking to be the strongest at such a young age.

"...Komekko. I'm going to go help Yunyun now. So you—"

I looked up at the sky as I spoke, trying to pinpoint the nearest location where there was fighting. There was a flash not far away. I crouched down so I was looking into Komekko's eyes.

"Run for the place that light came from just now. There will be grown-ups there. The monsters in the sky are looking for something; I don't think they'll be hostile to you. Besides, if you made it all the way to the tomb with everything that was going on, I know you'll be all right. Try to be inconspicuous. Stay out from under the lights if you can and hide whenever you—"

"Uh-uh! I'm coming, too!" Komekko said forcefully.

"...Do you understand? I'm going to go fight. Even your strong, cool sister might not win this time. So..."

Even as I tried to talk her out of it, Komekko balled up her little fist in front of her chest and said hotly, "I'll fight, too! I'll get back the food they stole!"

That made me worry a little about her future, but it was also greatly heartening.

As we retraced our steps, I kept saying, "Now, listen! You have to stay close to me!"

"Got it!"

"You must not immediately launch yourself at the monster who has Ink! Let me get her back for us! You understand?!"

"Got it! I'll try to hold back!"

"Don't tell me you'll *try*; tell me you won't!"

"Got it!"

Was this really going to be okay? Honestly, I had serious doubts. But even so, it was probably safer than sending my kid sister off by herself right now.

…I've made up my mind.

I wouldn't give up on Explosion. I didn't care if it took me years, decades—I *would* learn it.

I was just taking a bit of a detour.

Yes, just a small change of plans…

4

"*Blade of Wind*!"

Yunyun shouted the words and slashed through the air with her hand, causing a gust of wind. Little eddies turned into blades, cutting one of the monsters out of the sky.

Intermediate magic couldn't usually inflict fatal hits; it must have been thanks to Yunyun's innate magical power. I would expect no less from the second most capable person besides me.

Komekko and I stood apart, watching Yunyun fighting her valiant battle.

"Sis, aren't we going?"

"Just hold on, Komekko. Your ever-intelligent sister has noticed something. There's no need for me to learn Advanced Magic. We only have to survive to get out of this place."

As I spoke, I sized up the situation.

…I was not being a coward. Certainly not.

If, instead of consuming the huge amount of skill points necessary for Advanced Magic, I could skate by with Intermediate Magic as Yunyun had done, that would be ideal.

Yunyun was pressing her advantage. These monsters didn't leave corpses, so it was hard to say exactly how many Yunyun had defeated, but I recalled that when I had left, there had been six of them. Now, there was only a single one.

Yunyun had set Ink at her feet and was standing over her to protect her.

"…This is bad indeed. It looks as if Yunyun may defeat them all by herself."

"? Is that bad? Is Yunyun not allowed to beat them all?"

"She is not. If she did that, then all my summoning up resolve and turning back would be for—"

Then it happened. As if in answer to my prayers, seven more monsters came dancing out of the night sky.

Perfect! This was my opportunity to rush in and rescue Yunyun in return for what she had done for me.

"My name is—"

"My name is Komekko! She who is entrusted with watching the house and slyest demon of the little sisters of the Crimson Magic Clan!"

Komekko took the wind straight out of my sails.

"Komekko! You… You naughty child, how dare you steal your sister's big moment?!"

"Not sorry."

"K-Komekko!"

"Hey! Why are you two here?! I thought you ran away!" Yunyun shouted at us without ever taking her eyes off the monsters as they landed one after another.

"Surely you don't think that I, of all people, could run away, leaving myself indebted to my self-proclaimed rival," I said.

"Will you stop with this 'self-proclaimed' business already? And anyway, I'm a real wizard who's learned real magic now! I'm not a pretend, wannabe wizard like you anymore, Megumin!"

"A pretend wizard! Ooh, now you've gone and done it, you *intermediate* magic–user!"

"Don't call me that like it's a bad thing!"

As we argued, the last of the previous group of monsters lunged at Yunyun. She had never taken her eyes off it even while we were fighting, so she scooped up Ink in one hand, rolling away in a dodge. With her free hand, she whipped out her dagger and flung it at the enemy.

Maybe it was just luck, maybe, but her knife lodged cleanly in the monster's throat.

"Fweeee!" The monster clutched at its throat, making a sound like a flute as it collapsed to the ground and vanished in a puff of black smoke.

That convinced the newly arrived monsters to focus their attacks on Yunyun!

"Looks like you're in quite the fix, Yunyun, you *intermediate* magic–user! I, who am about to become a user of *advanced* magic, shall deal with these small fry in one swift stroke!"

"What?! Megumin, what brought that on?!" Yunyun jumped to her feet, holding her free hand up toward the sky as she spoke. "Why do you think I even learned Intermediate Magic…?!"

"From this day forth, I no longer consider you self-proclaimed but magnanimously recognize you as my true rival! And I refuse to be indebted to my rival! What's that? You were hoping to steal a march on me by graduating first? You know, I think I recall you wanted us to graduate together! And with this, we shall—"

"Fireball!!!"

"Huh?! Hey…!!"

Yunyun didn't even let me finish but launched a ball of fire at the monsters. No doubt it was imbued with considerable magical power: It detonated among the group of enemies with a force one would never have expected from intermediate magic, filling the area with an earsplitting roar!

The seven monsters that had come down from the sky turned into black smoke.

Yunyun made sure they were all gone, and then she slumped to the ground, probably out of magic.

I rushed over to her.

"Now you...don't have to learn Advanced Magic, Megumin...!" she said with a triumphant smile.

"...Some kind of a girl you are. And after you tried so hard to discourage me from learning Explosion— Why did you change your mind?" As I spoke, I pulled Yunyun to her feet, supporting her on my shoulder.

"I d-d-didn't change my mind... I still don't think you should learn Explosion, but I just couldn't stand to see you give up on your dream because of something like this... And! And! Since I went and learned Intermediate Magic because of you, I wanted to make sure you paid me back properly! I've never gotten a chance before to have you be in debt to me!"

"In recompense, I will help your poor, immobilized, magic-less self get back to your home, and then we will be even."

"Huh?!"

Komekko ran past the two of us to grab Ink. My sister's crimson eyes shimmered as she stared at the cat. I'd like to think she was overjoyed that Ink was safe.

"Come on, Megumin—I actually took Intermediate Magic to help you; there's no way we can be even just because you walked me home!"

"You are most contrary. You have used all your MP and can't move, so what if I left you here and some more monsters came along and ate you? It would not be an exaggeration to say that you owe your very life to me, Yunyun. So you have saved me once, and I have saved you once, no?"

"That's the dumbest logic! I risked my life in a huge fight with a bunch of monsters, and you..."

Suddenly, Yunyun stopped upbraiding me.

I followed her gaze, and then I, too, went silent.

"Sis, there's a bunch of those flying guys! Sis, are they edible? Can we eat them?" Komekko asked excitedly as we looked up at a flock of monsters dense enough to blot out the night sky.

5

I feel like I've done nothing but run today.

"M-Megumin, ow! I think my toe boxes are going to break off!" Yunyun complained tearfully from my back.

"That is too bad! I might argue that there is not much I can do about the difference in our heights! If your feet hurt so much, then grow shorter!"

"Okay, Yunyun, I'll hold your feet!"

I was pulling Komekko along and had the MP-less, immobilized Yunyun on my back as I dashed as fast as I could down the dark night path.

"Eeeyow-ow-ow! Komekko, don't! If you hold both my feet, I'll end up arched like a shrimp!"

"What are you both doing? This is an emergency! Please don't toss and fight on my back! Do you want me to leave you here?"

The horde of flying monsters swooped overhead even as we argued.

…Where did they all come from and why?

As if in answer to my question, magic lanced up toward the sky all around us.

By the time we realized what was happening, the villagers unleashing their magic on the monsters had closed the distance.

In other words, the monsters hadn't gathered together. They had been chased here, and we just happened to be in the middle of it.

"I guess this is where they're corralling the monsters," I said.

"So they're chasing the monsters right to the tomb of the Dark God?! Why would they…? Are they hoping to get them in one place and seal them up all at once?"

…That made sense. As Yunyun said, perhaps the adults meant to seal up the creatures in one fell swoop or otherwise blast them away with a single terrific volley of firepower.

Which meant we needed to be out of here the moment we could.

Easy enough to say, but…

"…Yunyun. If you have always wanted to say those most famous words, now is your chance. Go ahead: 'Forget about me; save yourselves!'"

"*D-don't* forget about me! You said yourself! You said you would get me home safely, and then we would be even!"

Curse me and my big mouth…!

I went along, Yunyun in tow, to the sickening cries of monsters overhead. Truthfully, even advanced magic would probably not have saved us against so many enemies.

We kept away from the lamps, moving through the shadows and praying they didn't see us.

And right then…

"Mrrrow."

Ink let out a little meow from where Komekko was holding her.

It was very, very little, but it was enough. The monsters fixed immediately on our position.

But that told me what was going on!

"Komekko! Throw that fur ball as high in the sky as you can!"

"What are you talking about?! Megumin, have you gone crazy?!"

"I finally got my food back! I can't give her away!"

"Komekko, you too?!"

…Gods above.

To think it took me—*me*—so long to realize it!

Those monsters must have attacked our house because they were looking for Ink. The school field trip had been the same. The monster had ignored all the other students there and come straight for me, the one carrying Ink.

Komekko had been playing with the pieces of the Dark God's seal on all those trips out of the house. And then one day she suddenly came home with this fur ball. The sightings of the Dark God's servants started about the same time. And with just one little meow, Ink was able to get their collective attention.

All these facts led to just one conclusion—!

"Owww, my head hurts! My brain can't think anymore! It's gone into self-protection mode...!"

"Megumin, what *are* you babbling about?! This is no time for escapism, okay?!"

Yunyun's words brought me back, and I took stock of our situation afresh.

The monsters in the sky were all zeroed in on us now. I would have liked to simply offer up Ink, but...

"Sis, look at all that chicken! Let's get a bunch of it and take it home!" My little sister—definitely a big deal in the making—offered this suggestion with a huge smile even as Ink trembled in her arms.

With Komekko's admiring eyes fixed on me, I set Yunyun down, looked at the sky, and pulled out my Adventurer's Card.

"M-Megumin?" Yunyun whispered apprehensively from the ground. Magic flew into the air, spell after spell, not far away.

I would learn Advanced Magic and buy us some time. If I fired a spell into the air at this distance, somebody would have to notice and come running.

"Sis, what's wrong? Your eyes are redder than usual."

Yes, of course they were. In the grip of such strong emotion, how could they not be?

"Yunyun, you stay with Komekko."

I looked at the sky and began to whip up the magical power within me. I had never cast a spell in my life, but my Crimson Magic Clan instincts told me how to wield the magical power that coursed through my body.

The servants of the Dark God circled warily above, not landing; maybe they thought we had Ink hostage. But I could tell they wouldn't wait forever; the slightest thing could provoke the burgeoning horde into a sudden and merciless assault.

The slightest thing such as, for example, a magic attack from me.

It's all right. I've made up my mind.

"M-Megumin, I think they're just watching us. Maybe we can wait until the adults get here…!"

I will have no regrets. I can keep striving for my goal.

"Sis, your eyes…" Komekko, still holding Ink, looked up at me anxiously. I patted her head as if to tell her it was all right.

Then, screwing my resolve to the sticking point, I raised my Adventurer's Card to select Advanced Magic.

When I looked at the card, I briefly froze.

Then, unable to restrain myself, I started laughing.

"Wh-what's going on?! Megumin, have you really lost your mind this time?!"

"Sis broke!"

"Th-that is most impolite! Both of you!"

Even as I shot back at them, though, I didn't take my eyes off my card.

I have the skill points.

I had all the points I needed to learn Explosion.

6

It was the magic I had worked for all my life, even knowing how foolish it was.

"Sis, you're shaking! You're quaking!"

"M-M-M-Megumin?! What is this?! What's happening?! What advanced-magic spell are you planning to use?! Even the village grown-ups don't look like this when they're using magic! Tell me what kind of spell this is!"

It was the incantation I had recited every day without fail since learning it by heart so long ago.

The air around me began to change in response to the magical energy I'd summoned, answering the words of the spell I was weaving together.

Static electricity ran around me; nearby scenery grew hazy.

It made sense; not only was I about to use magic for the very first time, the magic I was going to use was the spell that boasted the highest degree of difficulty: Explosion. Most likely, I couldn't quite channel all my magical energy into the spell, and some of it was escaping into the air around me, causing strange phenomena.

As I recited the incantation, memories went through my head.

I recalled needing just one more point to get Explosion.

Then I remembered wringing the neck of the Duxion that appeared in the park just after Yunyun and I had argued. That must have caused my level to go up and gained me the point I needed.

Perhaps sensing that something out of the ordinary was happening, the servants of the Dark God began to screech in their unearthly voices.

I knew that each word of the incantation that activated a magic spell consumed magical energy. And although I was confident in my supply of MP, I nonetheless felt a trickle of sweat. Explosion was known for consuming more magical energy than any other spell, and many who learned it simply lacked the innate energy to use it.

That was what the textbook had said anyway, but I was a member of the Crimson Magic Clan. How could I fail to cast the spell? I shook my head and kept chanting.

And when I had finally finished…in the palm of my hand, a small light shined.

…*I did it.*

In order to give birth to this tiny light, I had worked and struggled since I was a child, and I'd finally learned this spell.

I didn't yet have a staff to multiply the power of my magic. If I released my explosion now, it would probably be only half as strong as it could be.

And yet, even so.

"Yunyun. Komekko. Get on the ground and keep your heads down."

I was sure I could clear away the crowd of monsters jostling above us in a single blast.

Yunyun dragged her weakened body over to Komekko, holding my little sister in her arms as they both lay on the ground. She seemed to know what I had in mind.

The light in my hand was as hot as if it was on fire, yet it also had a pleasant pressure, like a massive power shrunk down to a small size.

It's all right. It's me. I can control this, I told myself as I looked up at the sky.

Explosion, the spell I had been waiting and hoping for for so long.

Explosion, the magic I had always been smitten with.

Explosion, for which I had been willing to risk my life.

Humanity's greatest and last resort, which, with a direct hit, could annihilate a dragon or a demon, even perhaps a god or the Demon King.

The image that had been burned into my mind as a child, I would now re-create with my own hand—

"My name is Megumin! Greatest genius of the Crimson Magic Clan and wielder of Explosion! This spell! This spell is all I have sought, and I have finally obtained it! This is the day I shall never forget! …Take this!!" I opened my eyes wide, thrust out my hand with the ball of light, and shouted—

"*Explooosion*!!!"

A flash lanced from my hand through the flock of monsters. Then it vanished, almost as if it had been absorbed into one of their bodies.

*　　*　　*

A beat later, there was a radiant flash, and then great flowers bloomed in the night sky—!

"Aaaahhhhhhhh! Eeeeeeek!!"

"—!!"

"Waaah-ha-ha-ha-ha-ha! This is it; this is what I so longed to see! What a blast! What destructive power! What a glorious feeling of release!"

While Yunyun screamed and hugged Komekko, I myself was in the highest of spirits, quite oblivious to the blowback and the roar that surrounded us.

The force of the explosion tore up the trees directly beneath it by the roots; I was of course tossed helplessly to the ground. The storm of wind produced by the immense magical energy, along with an overwhelming force and tremendous pressure no creature could stand against, wiped out the monsters in the sky.

I gazed up from where I had been tossed onto my back. My body was limp from using up my MP, but I couldn't take my eyes off the sky until the smoke cleared.

When I was finally able to see what was up there, the answer was... nothing. Not a single monster. The huge crowd of enemies was gone without a trace.

"...Wh-wh-what in the world...? Is this explosion magic...? *Amazing... Strong...* Those words can't even describe it... To wreak this sort of destruction without even a staff to focus and multiply its power... No wonder it's known as the strongest magic. I think... I think I have just the smallest inkling of why you were so taken by it, Megumin."

Yunyun sounded astonished by the sheer destructive power of Explosion. I couldn't muster up the enthusiasm to reply, though; I just rolled over. Apparently, all my MP hadn't quite been enough even for just that one blast, and it had consumed a considerable amount of my stamina as well.

After casting my spell, I was completely and totally vulnerable.

In other words, if I meant to become an adventurer, I would need to find friends who would protect me after I had used up all my MP and strength. I had always been known as the genius, and I had been convinced that I could handle everything by myself, but now Yunyun had rescued me once, and I could see that I was going to need faithful friends going forward.

I had been so sure that I would be all right by myself. But I guess there are some things you can't do on your own. I would have to be sure not to forget what had happened today. I would have to be sure always to treasure my friends and companions.

I could hear the village adults in the distance, clearly frantic. I thought of my future companions, the ones whose faces I couldn't even see yet...

And then, yielding to the fatigue, I closed my eyes.

"Awww!! Sis, you vaporized all the chickens!"

7

Several days later.

I gather that after the adults saw my explosion and came running, it was chaos.

After all, they arrived to find the chief's daughter and me collapsed on the ground, Komekko standing there with Ink in her hands as if to protect us.

I, still asleep, was carried back to my house; the next day, our teacher interrogated Yunyun and me about what had happened and gave us a severe scolding.

I explained only about having come home to find the door smashed in and Komekko missing and that Yunyun and I had gone to find her.

And that brought us to the present. A new problem had come up in the village.

"…Hey, Megumin. What are we going to do?" Yunyun asked expressionlessly.

"…………" I answered with silence.

Our teacher informed us that, since we had learned magic, a graduation ceremony would be held for the two of us on the weekend and that we were not to come to school other than to attend it.

That left us several days without much to do, and we passed the hours in the park next to my house.

"……Hey, Megumin."

This time I turned pointedly away.

Yunyun walked around me until I was facing her again, then she leaned in very, very close, as if to say that I wouldn't get away this time. "………Hey, Megumin. What are we going to dooooo?!"

I closed my eyes, blocked my ears to Yunyun's question, and crouched down on the ground.

"This is no time to pretend you can't hear me! Answer me! Bukkororii said… What did he call her? The goddess of manipulation and revenge, whose very name has been forgotten?! He said that's the seal that's been broken! And that the place that *was* sealed is the one where you fired off your magic! And that nobody knows where the goddess went now that she's free! So what are we going to do?! Come on—tell meeee!"

She pounded on my shoulders as I resolutely continued to pretend I couldn't hear her.

Though I would have liked to go on simply ignoring reality, there was one thing I had to correct. "Yunyun, wait just a moment, please. When you put it like that, someone could be misled into thinking that it was I who unsealed that seal."

"Misled? That's what happened! Bukkororii warned us that there were all kinds of dangerous things sleeping in this area! And you went and used Explosion right on top of it! And the overflow from all that magic broke the seal!"

Yunyun was insistent, but I retorted, "The adults seem to have taken a different view of things, have they not? They believe that the unsealed Dark God summoned the nameless goddess and challenged her to battle. The goddess emerged victorious and wiped out the Dark God's servants with that explosion, then disappeared who knows where… That's what they say…"

"Well, they're completely wrong! It was because of your magic spell, and you know it!"

No one in the village would have imagined that Komekko had broken the seal. Nor did they know I had learned Explosion. Our teacher was the only person who knew exactly what spells we had learned.

If the adults found out that I had taken Explosion and that Yunyun had learned the inferior Intermediate Magic instead of Advanced Magic, they would have been so disappointed. Our teacher must have realized that, because he kindly said nothing about our magic to anyone. I had never given him much credit as an instructor, but maybe he really did have the interests of his students at heart.

But right now, there were more important things.

"Yunyun. I don't suppose *today*…"

"No! Of course not! Things are finally quieting down, and you want to go cause another problem?! Anyway, you went your entire life without being able to use Explosion, so surely you can put up with a few more days! …D-don't give me that sad look. There's no way, okay? This is for your own good, Megumin!" She didn't sound entirely convinced herself.

It had been days since I had experienced the emotional moment of casting Explosion. Yunyun had put a moratorium on my casting the spell. After our teacher had been willing to keep my new magic secret, it would have caused quite the stir for an explosion to go off near the village, or at least, so Yunyun said.

It was logical enough, I admit. But there's logic, and then there's…

"Yunyun, you know now how much I love and cherish Explosion, don't you?"

"W-well, yes. You love it so much that even people who just *see* your explosions sort of get it, don't you?"

If she understood that, then this conversation would be a quick one.

"Listen to me, Yunyun. My love of Explosion is such that if I had to choose between eating just one meal a day and being able to set off an explosion each day or having three square meals *plus snacks* but no explosions, I would gladly live with the single meal. And then after I had lived with it long enough to set off my explosion, I would be sure to eat the other two meals plus my snacks. That is how much I adore this spell."

"Huh... And I know how much you love to eat, Megumin...! ...? W-wait, what?! Say that again?! I think there was something funny there!"

Despite how flustered Yunyun was, I did understand how fraught it would be to go try out an explosion just now. I scratched the head of the little fur ball at my feet. "Eh, I suppose I can endure for a while. When at last I can no longer wait, I will immediately leave on my journey to encompass the whole world outside the village with my conflagrations."

"S-stop that! Don't even joke about that!"

I stood up and, hoping to change the subject, said, "In any case, there were no casualties this time, so it is all good. The truth may end up a bit twisted, but so long as the people of the village can accept it, what's the harm?"

I picked up the fur ball.

Yunyun looked at Ink, then cocked her head, her face full of conflicting emotions. "...Hey. What *is* the story with Ink anyway? Why did those creatures keep coming after her? Could she have something to do with the Dark God? I wonder why the Dark God's seal broke anyway. Do you really think some passing traveler did it as a prank, like the villagers say...?"

It seemed Yunyun had not quite grasped the true heart of the matter. I suppose it would be a rare person who simply guessed the truth: A child's curiosity had broken the seal. I myself would never have suspected Komekko if I hadn't done the same thing when I was her age.

I'd asked her about it at home, and it seemed I was right. I thought I should scold her for it, but my little sister had shown me the pieces with such an innocent smile, saying, "You wanna play, too?" that I found I couldn't say anything at all.

As for our house, the damage extended no farther than the front door, so we could live with it.

This little thing is the problem.

"She seems rather assertive. I might wish for a kitten to be a bit sweeter."

The servants of the Dark God had been looking for Ink, and when they had found her, they had held her almost delicately.

Was it possible she was actually...?

"Megumin, are you planning to keep that cat at your house? I—I mean... The way Komekko was looking at her..."

Yunyun didn't finish her thought aloud. I understood, though, exactly what she meant.

"An excellent question. True, leaving her at our house might put her at risk of becoming Komekko's next meal. But I don't think I could ask someone else to take her at this point, let alone release her into the wild..."

I held Ink up to look at her. She made no effort to resist or struggle.

Yunyun, looking on, clapped her hands. "That's it! Maybe you really should contract with her as your familiar. If she was your precious magical companion, even Komekko wouldn't..."

She trailed off as she spoke. But again, I understood what she was saying: Logic would probably not stop my sister, who lived primarily by her instincts.

A familiar, though. Hmm...

"...A wizard who has the Dark God for a familiar. That has a nice ring to it."

"? Megumin, did you say something?"

Yunyun hadn't caught my little whisper.

"Yes, I said it might be nice to have her for my familiar," I fudged. Then I smiled at the fur ball who might be much more than a fur ball.

Yunyun let out a relieved breath. But something occurred to me.

"That's right. If you are to be my familiar, then it will hardly do for you to go through life with a placeholder for a name."

"Huh?! You mean Ink can't be her real name?!"

"Certainly not. I would feel awful for her, being stuck with such a bizarre, tasteless name for her entire existence."

"Bizarre? Tasteless?!"

Yunyun appeared practically traumatized, but I ignored her; I focused on coming up with a name.

Ink, though, suddenly twisted around, almost as if to say she was happy the way she was.

"See?" Yunyun said. "I think even Ink likes her name just fine. Anyway, she's still a kitten. Don't you think it'll confuse her if we keep changing her name?" But as Yunyun tried to defend her choice of name, I had a brilliant idea.

"I've decided!" The confidence in my tone provoked a look of anxiety from Yunyun.

"Uh, Megumin. Ink's a girl, remember? So make sure you pick a nice, cute—"

But I interrupted her, addressing the familiar I held up in front of my face.

"Your name shall be Chomusuke. Yes, Chomusuke!"

My familiar, who had always done her own thing and might well be of far greater consequence than in our wildest dreams, shivered even harder than she ever had before.

The High-Level Demon and the Demonic Girl

"Yo, Komekko."

"Yo, Host!"

Host, carrying something, came in for a landing where I was standing by the tomb of the Dark God.

"It's been a while… What's all this anyway? Everything was real torn up around the tomb, including some of the trees. What in the world happened?"

"They say the Dark God came back to life. Then it summoned the nameless goddess, and they had a big fight, but the Dark God lost and was destroyed."

Host dropped the thing in his hand. It was a cage with a big hen and some chicks.

"No waaaaaaaaay!"

"That's what the grown-ups said."

Host hung his head in disappointment, but I was more worried about the birds in the cage.

"H-how did Lady Wolbach's seal…? Argh, I take my eyes off that thing for *one* minute…… Huh? It's weird, though. If Lady Wolbach's other half was destroyed, I shouldn't still be here in this world…"

I crouched down by the cage and was looking inside when Host exclaimed, "That's it! That must mean Lady Wolbach's other half *wasn't* destroyed! It's gotta be wandering around lost somewhere.

I better hurry up and find it, keep it safe…" He glanced at me. "…So, uh, well. That's the story. I guess this is good-bye, kid… I don't need no more living sacrifices. You can keep those."

"Great, we'll have the hen for dinner and the chicks can be for Chomusuke!"

"You're gonna eat 'em?! All right, that'd be no good for your, y'know, moral education, so I think I'll keep these. Who the heck is Chomusuke anyway?"

"She's an inky-black magical creature, 'bout this big. Wanna see her?"

"Pass. She, like, a kitten or something? You oughta give her a better name than that… Bah, whaddaya expect from the Crimson Magic Clan…"

He spread the wings on his back.

"…Are you going somewhere?"

"Huh? Weren't you listening to a word I said? I'm gonna go find Lady Wolbach… Aww, don't pull that face. I've got no choice. Anyway, I… You're Crimson Magic Clan, right?" I nodded. "Well, I've got a feeling you're gonna be a wizard to watch out for when you grow up. So listen. If I ever end my contract with Lady Wolbach… If you're able to summon me, then I'd be happy to contract with you as your familiar."

"Really?!"

"That's only if you can summon me! Calling on a high-level demon like the great and wonderful yours truly—it might be darn near impossible for you…"

I just cocked my head at him. Host flapped his wings and floated into the sky, but then he settled back down to earth and met my eyes.

"Yeah, it might be impossible, but… I do think you have the makings of a Demon Master. You might really be able to summon even the likes of me."

"I'll do my best!"

With another "Maybe, maybe not," Host mussed my hair. "See ya, Komekko! You go become a great big wizard! My name is Host! High-level demon and servant of Lady Wolbach!"

"And my name is Komekko! She who is entrusted with watching the house and slyest demon of the little sisters of the Crimson Magic Clan! And she who plans to one day work with Host!"

I threw my cape, which had been dragging on the ground, out behind me, posing for Host. He laughed out loud and then gave a mighty flap of his wings, flying away from the village.

He might have complained a lot, but in the end, he always brought me food. He had been my first friend, and now I watched him go until he disappeared in the distance, waving at him all the while.

Epilogue

Inside the dim shop, the proprietress offered me a chair.

We were in the shop of the village's fortune-teller, Soketto. Just when I was starting to think everything had been neatly tied up, she personally asked me to come over.

"…Well. Things have been a little rough for you, huh, Megumin?" Soketto smiled from behind her table.

I still didn't know why I was there. What did she mean by "rough"? Was she talking about me being chased around by the servants of the Dark God?

"…Be sure to buy your little sister a proper toy."

"?!" I quaked with shock, eliciting a giggle from Soketto.

"Don't worry—I won't tell anyone. Fortune-tellers know how to keep a secret. I didn't call you here today about that."

I let out a breath of relief as I looked at Soketto, who had her hand on her crystal ball. "Then why did you call me here? Oh, is it Bukkorori-rii? Has that man done something again? Yes, I have been acquainted with him for quite a long time, but I'm afraid complaining to me about him will not do you much good."

"That's not it, either. I see him hanging around outside the shop sometimes, but he hasn't caused me any trouble." Soketto beckoned me to come closer. "Today…I wanted to tell your fortune." She smiled.

"Tell my fortune? About what? So you know, I don't have much interest in love."

"Well, isn't that a shame. But it is what it is. I just wanted to see where you would go in the future. Call it a fortune-teller's intuition. I think you're going to do big things."

"So you're driven by simple curiosity? Very well, I don't mind. But if it turns out I will have an unhappy future, I don't want to know too many details."

"Ah, but the future can be changed, you know. Giving advice on how to avoid an unhappy outcome is my job." Soketto placed her hand happily on her crystal ball and began channeling magic into it. "...Hmm. First, it seems you intend to leave this village and go to a town called Axel, yes? I see, I see. And there, after many trials, you will meet wonderful companions. They will be extremely intelligent... Well...hmm...intelli...gent......? A-anyway, they'll have wonderful personalities... H-huh...? This boy, he... Ugh..."

"What is it?! Tell me—I must know! What do you see about my companions?! Are they brilliant, diligent, kind people?!"

Soketto looked away and didn't say a word.

"Helping people avoid unhappy fates is your job, is it not?! Out with it!" I was shaking her shoulders by this point when suddenly, her expression changed.

"...Now, this. Huh, Megumin, you *will* be blessed with good companions."

"Which is it?! You said the future can be changed! Now I'm starting to have second thoughts about going to Axel...!"

Soketto smiled bitterly. "It would be troublesome if *this* future changed. I think I'll keep quiet."

"Tell me! Now I *really* want to know!"

Her smile changed to one of amusement, but that was all I seemed to get out of her.

"...Mm, you certainly will do big things together. A catastrophe looms over this village, and when it comes, you guys will be involved somehow."

"This fortune seems very open-ended… I had heard your fortunes were very specific and frequently accurate, Soketto."

Soketto just shrugged and smiled. "The catastrophe in the village is going to have something to do with me, too, and fortune-tellers can't see things that involve themselves." She ran her hand gently over the surface of the crystal ball. I guess her point was that life wasn't so easy as to allow someone who could see the future to simply manipulate their own.

A catastrophe that would involve Soketto… From all the recent fuss to the various dangerous things sealed away in this village, the possibilities seemed nearly endless.

"I suppose it could involve an assault by the Demon King's army," she said. "Though I hear Bukkororii is getting together some weird group just in case that happens."

She must have meant his "Red-Eye Dead Slayers."

………*Huh?*

Come to think of it, when Bukkororii had asked about his future girlfriend, the crystal ball hadn't shown anything. And apparently, Soketto couldn't see anything involving herself, so…?

"I guess Bukkororii isn't that bad a guy, if he would just get a job. And if he could stop stalking people and doing all that weird stuff, I'm sure he'd find someone nice… Are you okay, Megumin? What are you grinning about?"

"Oh, nothing. I was just thinking sometimes it's difficult to strike a balance."

Balance? Soketto seemed to be thinking as she cocked her head. "Anyway, the only thing I'll say is to look forward to your time in Axel… You want advice? Stay strong, no matter how much sexual harassment you may endure."

"I'm going to be sexually harassed by someone?! You mean one of my comrades?! Are you *sure* these are good people?!"

*   *   *

I left the shop, Chomusuke's claws digging into my flesh where she was perched on my shoulder. It hurt a little, but that wasn't what was bothering me most at that moment. Here I hadn't even set out on my journey, and I had already received some troubling news. Maybe I should just shut myself away in this village...

"Anyway, I guess I have to save up enough money to get out of here first. I will worry about it after that," I told myself, then took Chomusuke from my shoulder into my arms.

Even if my companions turned out to be good-for-nothings, I simply had to support them.

I have two goals.

One was to show that woman my Explosion. And the other...

This world crawled with monsters. With bounty heads and demons.

I had something to prove to such ruffians.

I would show them that now that I knew Explosion, it was I who was the strongest.

Be my opponent a Dark God or even the Demon King himself—

For some reason, I felt Chomusuke tremble in my arms.

I hugged her tighter, my red eyes shining.

Yes, I would let loose an explosion on the bosses of this world—!

STAFF

Author/Natsume Akatsuki

This work is a Konosuba spin-off originally
serialized on Sneaker Bunko's official website.
It's not like you have to read this thing to
understand the main series, but it'll give
you some extra grins.
Like, it turns out that character is actually…!
…I'm out of pages? …Thank you, everyone who
was involved in making this book—and my
deepest thanks to my readers!

Illustrations/Kurone Mishima

I got so excited while reading this, more than
once. Here's to another explosion on
your daily life next time!

Article

Arue

Jacket

Yuko Yuriya (Mushikago Graphics)
Nanafushi Nakamura (Mushikago
Graphics)

Editing

Kadokawa Sneaker Bunko Editorial Section

CAST

Megumin
Yunyun
Komekko
Chomusuke

Arue
Kaikai
Sakiberii
Dodonko
Nerimaki
Funifura

Pucchin
Bukkororii
Soketto

SPECIAL THANKS

Host
Kyouya Mitsurugi
The People of Crimson Magic Village

An Explosion on This Wonderful World! Megumin's Turn

—END—

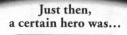

Just then,
a certain hero was…

I'm looking for the beautiful goddess who's supposed to be sealed up in this village.

She made tracks…just the other day.

Huh?!

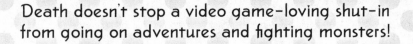
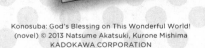

Read the light novel that inspired the hit anime series!

-Starting Life in Another World-

Also be sure to check out the manga series!

AVAILABLE NOW!

www.YenPress.com